Hot Lips

Hot Lips

Joe Baumann

CURIOUS CURLS PUBLISHING

The following stories appeared in different form in the following publications:
"Hot Lips" in *Arkana Magazine*
"Glacier" in *Platform Review*
"Adam" in *Chaffin Journal*
"Honeycomb" in *Santa Clara Review*
"Frequent Flyer" in *Litro Magazine*
"Mort" in *Vast Chasm*

Curious Curls Publishing
CuriousCurlsPublishing.com
@CuriousCurlsPub

Baumann, Joe.
Hot Lips / Joe Baumann.
ISBN 978-1-958373-02-6 (paperback)
Print: January 2023

Cover Illustrations by Dusty Marchand

For Giles, Linus, and Dickory, three cats who made no
contribution to this book except to distract me from writing it.

Table of Contents

Hot Lips

They called him Hot Lips, not because he had a beautiful mouth—he did—but because he could breathe fire. Every belch after chugging Natural Light came with a small burst of flame. Every exhalation while he ate triple-pepper spicy chicken wings or grilled cheese from the campus dining hall was like lighting a blow torch. If he coughed, the blue heat of a Sterno canister flashed between his teeth. He could make smoke seep from his nose if he held his breath long enough, and he could puff out little rings of flame like people did with cigar smoke. When he showed strangers what he could do, they would clap, then go back to playing beer pong or Fuck the Dealer or slip into the crowd of drunk kids sloshing beer from their Solo cups as they danced to the heavy rap music his Phi Kappa Gamma fraternity brothers played at parties. No one ever asked him his real name.

The fire didn't hurt, he said. It was like a feathery tickle, a relieving scratch along an itchy patch of skin. Yes, if he went too long between exhaled flames he started to feel weird. It built up, like a belch waiting to get out.

People asked how he slept, if he had to worry about roasting his pillows or setting his sheets on fire.

No, he told them. He breathed like a normal person most of the time. He was pretty normal, he said.

This made people laugh, even though he was being serious.

Sometimes, people wanted him to open his mouth wide, jaw stretched to the precipice of dislocation. But he could see their disappointment when all they saw was a set of normal—and perfectly white—teeth, a regular tongue, a standard uvula and epiglottis. Then they would wander away, watching his tricks with vague disinterest. He felt each dismissal like a tiny, bloodless stab.

He spent lots of time at the college gym, lifting weights and running HIIT sprints on treadmills. He filled barbells with forty-five pound plates and let out small bursts of flame as he pressed the weight up, feeling power in his chest. As he ran, he let out heaves of fire that licked toward the mirrors along the wall, leaving small circles of soot he wiped away with his towel so the student workers didn't glare at him. He wore tank tops because he liked the way his shoulders swelled with blood and lactic acid. He'd been blessed with Swedish bone structure and thick blond hair by his Nordic parents, and when he told people about his background they laughed, wondering how someone with roots in such a cold place could be so hot.

Some girls wanted him to go down on them, to know if the heat of his tongue would do new, spicy things. His friends laughed about paying him for blow jobs, his mouth warm and welcoming, and he laughed with them, never admitting that he had, in fact, never gotten a blow job of his own. He wasn't afraid of sex, didn't view his virginity as something pure and porcelain and needing delicate safekeeping. But he always saw himself as a farce, a thing drunk sorority girls and his fraternity brothers laughed at, well-intentioned joking that he was supposed be on the inside of.

Hot Lips was voted fraternity vice president at the end of his sophomore year, which meant he got to share a private bathroom with the president and had a room of his own; he wasn't subjected to a tiny space with bunked beds made of rough-hewn two-by-fours etched with the fraternity numbers of everyone who'd slept on them, and he didn't have to contend with roommates bringing home girls, wasn't subject to their sex noises while pretending to be asleep, didn't have to avoid them by passing out on a couch in the foyer. He didn't have to cram his clothes into a doorless closet with makeshift shelves that fell down under the weight of too many hangers. Hot Lips kept his room clean; when he moved in, he painted the walls a light lilac and didn't pin up any cheap posters of beer bottles and half-naked women, nor did he hijack and hang stolen bar signs. He vacuumed the throw rug every weekend with a Hoover he kept in his closet, and he even Windexed his windows and his flat-screen television. His room smelled oceanic and beachy thanks to expensive air fresheners he plugged into the outlets near the floor. The fraternity liked to feature his room during tours, ignoring the crammed, gross rooms that the rest of the guys occupied. Hot Lips would be sitting at his computer during rush week, playing video games or, more often, writing something in a notebook, "Poems," his friends would say. Hot Lips would smile and lean back, not arguing with them.

He was a good vice president, staying sober during big parties to make sure no one called the cops and issued them a noise violation. Whenever drunk sorority girls started screeching on the lawn or in the basement stairwell that led up into the side yard, he let out a warm, glowing breath and asked if people would please go back inside. He had a nice smile—those beautiful lips, the color of cherry, those white teeth, like fresh snow—and people complied, asked if he would like to dance.

He did like to dance, but he always said no, imagining his body up against strangers. Hot Lips had dreams of dancing, sexy bodies slithering around him, pawing at his arms and his chest, which was always stripped bare in his dreams, the hands touching him as hot as the fire that churned in his throat. These faceless bodies whispered into his ears, things like, "Light me up," and "I want to burn, please." They would reach down between his legs, and he would shiver awake, erection throbbing under his body weight.

Hot Lips knew that everyone knew of his solitude. They knew, too, that it would one day get broken apart, that someone would show up and free him of his virginal loneliness. What none of his fraternity brothers knew was that it would be a kid with hair dyed the blue-green of a pond with matching eyes. Clive Lewindowski stumbled into their house on a Friday night early in spring semester of Hot Lips' junior year, four girls from his dorm in tow. Clive had been heavily recruited by every fraternity when he rushed in the fall; rumor had it he was excellent at sports and would boost the chances of his new house winning the annual intramural competition for the next four years. But Clive didn't join anywhere that semester, telling recruitment chairs that he needed more time to decide what was right for him. No one wanted to frighten him away, so all of the fraternities welcomed him with warm greetings and slaps on the back whenever he showed up to their parties. It didn't hurt that girls followed him around, a cluster of freshman women, some of whom had joined sororities and some who had not, all chasing after him as he party-hopped.

Hot Lips was playing a game of beer pong in the house foyer when Clive walked in, stomping his snow-crusted shoes along the welcome mat on the front porch before heaving himself inside, shaking flakes from his thick hair. Clive and Hot Lips had not met in the fall because Hot Lips had come down with the flu during rush and had kept to his room, ignoring the wafting voices that floated up through the air vents during the tours and meet and greet. Now, though, Hot Lips found himself unable to stop staring at Clive, who was tall and wide, his limbs bearing the sinewy strength of a tennis player. His eyes darted around the room, taking in the scene of the party, which was small thanks to the weather, clusters of co-eds chatting while gripping their beer cans, some sitting on ratty couches around rickety tables where they played drinking games. His eyes settled on Hot Lips, who missed a shot because he was distracted by Clive's hard gaze.

Clive wandered, his coterie of girls following him like a flock of gulls after an ice cream cone. He eventually settled at the beer pong table. Hot Lips felt the flame that raged in his throat grow harder, hotter, as if he was flaring with sickness. He and his partner had one cup left to make, and he threw three shots long before finally sinking the ping pong ball with a fluff of noise as it hit beery foam. His partner, a beanpole studying linguistics and psychology who was terrible at anything athletic except for the game they'd been playing, asked Clive if he wanted a turn. Hot Lips blinked at his partner, who shrugged and said he was too full to play anymore. With a burp that left a spark blinking off his teeth, Hot Lips said, "Okay." Clive nodded assent, and took the ball that Hot Lips held out toward him.

Clive smelled like the ocean, as if his hair had seeped into his pores. He said hello and offered a tight, strong handshake, his palms calloused. When Hot Lips introduced himself, Clive raised an eyebrow.

"That can't be your name."

"Nickname," Hot Lips said.

"What's your real name?"

"You don't want to know why they call me that?"

Clive dunked his ping pong ball in the cup of water meant for rinsing. "I'd like to know your actual name."

Hot Lips licked his lips, little flames buzzing at the edges. He let out a short breath, his teeth backlit by the light of his internal sun, and said, "Allen."

"Hi, Allen."

They played three games, first against two of the girls Clive had brought along. The girls were lucky to sink two of their ten cups before Clive, who shot with his arm reached up high like he was going to dunk it into a basketball hoop and swished the last cup, making four shots in a row to end the game. He offered Hot Lips a high five after every made shot, and Hot Lips let his hand linger against Clive's, his eyes sparkling with the heat that was usually concentrated in his mouth. They didn't lose that third game but instead gave up the table when Clive said he could use some fresh air. His gaggle of girls tried to follow, though two of them had split off to play King's Cup in the TV room, but he shook them off.

"Join me?" he said to Hot Lips.

They grabbed beers and marched outside, not to the front but to the deck at the back of the house, which was empty, its composite planks swept with a thin coating of snow. Neither Clive nor Hot Lips wore a coat, and both shivered, but they drank their cold beers, Hot Lips leaning against the porch rail while Clive blew into his hands and pulled a Zippo from his pocket.

"I don't smoke," he said, as if Hot Lips had accused him. "I just like the feel of the flame close to my skin. I'm always cold."

Hot Lips smiled, beer churning in his gut. His breath came out in puffs of condensation full of tiny flames like the butt-ends of fireflies. "I'm always hot."

"So I gathered," Clive said, "from the nickname."

"That's not really why they call me that."

"Then why do they?"

"You really don't know?"

"Should I?"

So Hot Lips showed him. He did all his tricks, pouring smoke from his nostrils, grinning so fire seeped between his incisors. He stuck out his tongue, letting a racetrack of cerulean heat screech down its center. Clive watched, eyes lidded. He crinkled his beer can with his fingers and drank. When Hot Lips was done, Clive nodded. "Impressive. What's it feel like?"

"It doesn't hurt."

"That's not what I asked." Clive pointed toward Hot Lips' chest, his stomach. "In there. What's it like in there?"

No one had ever asked, really. And not the way Clive was asking, looking him in the eye, not ready to move away now that the carnival sideshow had come to its conclusion. His eyes were shadowed by the darkness and the falling snow, but Hot Lips could feel their piercing color, the occluded algae-aquamarine that he'd memorized as they stood next to each other, just as he'd memorized Clive's cleft chin, the slight leftward lean of his nose, the thickness of his eyelashes like he was wearing mascara.

"It's like I've got a furnace," Hot Lips said.

"Sounds unpleasant."

"Sometimes it is."

"And other times?"

"Other times it's okay."

They drank their beers in silence. They could hear the party on the other side of the door, voices rising to outdo one another, the thrum of the music, now something country that Hot Lips knew the social chair must have turned on, twangy lyrics about red Solo cups that girls loved to scream. A car pulled into the house lot behind Clive, illuminating his ears and mussy hair.

"Would you like a tour?" Hot Lips said. "Of the upstairs?"

"I've seen it before," Clive said.

"Have you seen all of it?"

Clive raised an eyebrow, then shrugged and said, "I guess I haven't."

They went back inside, the heat blasting them in the face. Snow melted on Hot Lips' shoulders as he led the way to the second floor. They passed composites and pledge class paddles. Clive stopped on the landing between floors, staring at the one with Hot Lips' name on it. "At least they let you put the real thing on this," he said, running his fingers over the letters.

Hot Lips smiled. "There was some debate."

"I like Allen. It suits you better." Clive glanced at him. "Though you do have nice lips."

Hot Lips swallowed a warm breath.

"They ever smack you with this thing?" Clive asked.

"No," Hot Lips said, shaking his head. "I'm sure they do that at some schools, but not here."

"Good. You don't deserve that."

Hot Lips took the remaining stairs two at a time. The second floor was a giant horseshoe with a windowless, three-person bedroom in the center, called The Coffin because it received no natural light. The walls had been painted over winter break, a fresh, blank white, a trio of holes made by drunk idiots punching through the drywall, repaired and sanded over, and the effect was dizzying in its cleanliness; Hot Lips decided he would propose some kind of décor to interrupt the snowy glare.

Along the exterior of the horseshoe were half a dozen of the smaller rooms, each with scuffed hardwood floors and narrow desks and lofted beds. Most nights, people could come and go from the first floor to the second, but generally people stayed downstairs where communal beer was within close range. The second floor was quiet aside from the spilled hum of downstairs and the distant tinkle of the one or two occupied rooms. Many of the doors were closed, their occupants downstairs. One was cracked open, home to a sophomore who was constantly high, even though technically their leases forbade controlled substances. Everyone looked the other way so long as he smoked in the parking lot or went on drives and cleaned up his spilled bud immediately after rolling fresh joints. From behind the door of another room came the sound of whispering voices and the low hum of classic rock.

Hot Lips and the president lived in rooms on the left end of the horseshoe, larger and connected by a Jack-and-Jill bathroom for their use only; as Hot Lips explained to Clive as they approached, the door locked from the outside and in, using a key that only he and the president had copies of.

"Very elite," Clive said. "I've seen the communal bathroom. Have none of you heard of Comet?"

Hot Lips opened his bedroom door. He was grateful he'd cleaned that afternoon, gathering up discarded t-shirts and underwear and stuffing them into his hamper. He'd dusted his nightstand and straightened the books on his desk, secreted away stray pens and his highlighters that he'd been using to mark key terms in his poli-sci textbook.

"Smells nice," Clive said.

"Tropical sunset."

"Thoughtful. For the guests, I mean. I like the paint color. Do that yourself?"

Hot Lips nodded, then looked at Clive. He didn't seem anxious at all, any uncertainty or nerve buried behind those lake-like eyeballs. His hair was shiny in the overhead light, waves of muted blue like aquarium displays at the zoo meant to recreate the ocean floor.

"I don't get many guests," Hot Lips said.

"That's a shame." Clive's eyes traveled around the room, landing on the bed with its crisp hospital corners. "It's much nicer in here than the rest of the rooms."

"It's a perk."

"Of what?"

"Being vice president."

"Should I refer to you as Mr. Vice President?"

"No," Hot Lips said.

"VP Hot Lips?"

"Allen is fine."

"Good," Clive said, stepping close. Hot Lips could smell beer on his breath, as well as something briny. And something chilly, cool, like an ice pack. Clive leaned in close, his mouth at Hot Lips' ear. "I like Allen."

Hot Lips tried to think of something to say, but his lips felt like melted tar, his teeth soft as cheese. Clive didn't seem to notice, or care. He set a hand on Hot Lips' right shoulder, fingers pressing down as if his body was a piano and Clive an accomplished player.

The pressure was light, not demanding or leading, though Hot Lips wished Clive would take control, show and do whatever it was he wanted. He was tall, taller than Hot Lips by a few inches, his gaze aimed slightly downward, the tip of his nose glowing with grease in the light. Or maybe it was the heat of Hot Lips' breath pushing onto his body and stirring him with warmth.

Clive let out a breath that pushed toward Hot Lips' nose. Cool, as though he'd swallowed snow. Hot Lips shut his eyes and let the refrigerator air waft over him. He could hear the party below. He also felt a warmth in his throat, the soft heat that surrounded his heart and made its way up to his mouth, cresting the back of his tongue in a rising wave. What he never told anyone—hadn't even told Clive—was that the heat was equal parts unctuous and acidic, a delicious ambrosia and a nauseated days-old vodka taste in the back of his throat. That when he did his tricks, he was sometimes feeling joyous pleasure and also a horrified relief, releasing something both wonderful and toxic into the air that his friends and audience absorbed with glee regardless.

Hot Lips felt it coming, that horrible heat, and he opened his mouth to let it out, hoping for a gentle, quick stream of flame. But before he could do anything, Clive's lips were on his, Clive's tongue dancing carefully across his teeth, the salty ocean aroma purging any hint of smoke, and Hot Lips kissed him back, feeling something cool inside him as one of Clive's hands touched the back of his head, gently massaging the nape of his neck, dropping his temperature and wetting his mouth with something from a fresh spring. Hot Lips brushed Clive's cheek with his hand, and for the first time in a long time he felt like he was not going to burn up.

Meat Lover

Two guys playing beer pong recognized Clint as soon as he walked into the party.

"Holy shit," one of them shouted. "It's Meat Lover!"

Clint had appeared on a number of Food Network shows as a kid and won plenty of competitions that never made it on television. His track record was perfect, and that had earned him profiles in *The New York Times, Gastronomica,* and *Food and Wine.* They all wanted to know: how could a kid, a child, outdo pit masters and trained chefs? How had he, at seventeen, beaten Bobby Flay, and with a signature dish of simple pork chops to boot? Why was he able to braise, poach, broil, sauté, and roast better than the rest of the planet? Clint's answers were always coy, vague explanations about trusting his instincts, having a good palate and strong muscle memory regarding what worked and didn't. But how, his questioners wanted to know, was he so good at producing both cakes and lamb shank? Where did his ability to construct a delicate tiramisu and then a Huntsman pie come from? Clint always shrugged and said he was a quick study. Reporters called him a prodigy. One of his competitors once saw him whispering to a slab of baby back ribs and, on camera, called him Meat Lover, and the nickname stuck, showing up on chyrons and in profiles starting the day before he turned fifteen, when he won *Chopped: Grill Masters.*

What Clint didn't ever mention was that the foods told him what to do.

Clint was eight years old when the eggs he was frying for Mother's Day talked to him. His parents were still in bed; he and his dad had schemed the day before, father showing son how to work the burner, leaving the eggs and a non-stick skillet out overnight. They'd practiced once, when Clint's mom called it a night after drinking the two glasses of Malbec that she and Clint's dad consumed every Saturday evening. She taught fifth grade, and so even when summer was on the horizon, she was exhausted as the hour ticked past eight. Clint had helped his father cook the eggs perfectly, the yolks seeping out when their forks cut into the middles, a golden ambrosial goop.

Sun gleamed through the window above the sink as Clint worked, standing on a small stepstool for extra leverage. When he was older, he would wonder at the ridiculousness of his father thinking it was okay that an eight-year-old was working the buttons and knobs of a stove; how easy it would have been for Clint to burn himself, or to light an oven mitt on fire, or send spumes of smoke into the air that would set the smoke detector blaring. But as the eggs cooked, wobbly and wet albumin solidifying, he was thinking only of the look on his mother's face when he presented her with breakfast. He was about to prod the eggs when he heard a voice say, "Not just yet."

The voice was high and airy, coaxing and cajoling, gentle and bright like the yolks sputtering in the skillet. When his mom and dad, taking their first tentative bites, raised their eyebrows and glanced at one another, chewing and *mmm*-ing and going back for more, they asked, "What did you season this with?"

"Paprika," Clint said.

The question in both of their eyes: how did he even know what paprika was?

The eggs had suggested it, told him just how much to sprinkle atop: a little more, a little more, stop! And Clint, a good listener, did as he was told.

He asked his father that night if he could help with dinner, simple spaghetti and meatballs, which his father made every Sunday. While he left his father to manage the pasta—though it did start crowing at him when it wanted to be taken off the burner—Clint made the meatballs, following his father's recipe for the most part but easing off the panko when the beef clucked that enough was enough. The strings of ground meat coaxed him through adding salt and pepper and minced garlic, yodeling with glee as he rolled thick mounds the size of golf balls in his hands and spaced them out on the cooking sheet. Clint could hear them call out when it was time to turn them over, and even though his father tried to stop him, said they needed a few more minutes, Clint's insistence won out, and he helped his father press the meatballs gently with the spatula so they lifted and rolled, the beef cooing that he was doing a fantastic job. The meatballs went back in, and a few minutes later they called to be let out. Clint's mother, unaware of her son's hand in the manufacture of the meal, let out a satisfied groan after her first bite, extolling the meatballs in particular.

A month later, he entered his first kiddie cooking competition: hamburgers. He won, a unanimous decision.

The beer pong players paused their game to greet Clint, one screaming out, "Holy shit, you *are* Meat Lover," the other pulling a can of beer from a case of Budweiser sitting on the floor next to him and handing it to Clint without asking if he drank. Clint didn't, not really. He'd cooked with sherry and pinot noir and once vodka but had never really imbibed, even when he made beer can chicken, his father dutifully downing half of the Berliner Weisse. But now he was in college, so he took the can and sipped, a tentative gulp of sour liquid that he managed to swallow without coughing. He took another, his mouth already acclimating to the stinging taste, and then a third, by which point it went down as smooth as it ever would.

"You're really him, huh?" one of the beer pong players said. They were both taller than Clint, arms sinewy with lean muscle from the campus gym, one sporting a goatee and wispy chest hair that poked up out of his V-neck t-shirt. The other was clean-shaven, eyes the sparkling color of champagne. Clint caught a breath and drank some more, nodding.

"What the shit are you doing in this podunk town?" the one with the golden eyes said.

"I'm a freshman," Clint said, which made both of them laugh.

"Yeah," Goatee said, "but why here?"

"Shouldn't you be studying in France or something, or, like, schmoozing with Giada and Bobby?" his friend asked.

"Fuck that," Goatee said. "He beat Bobby! He should be teaching at, like, L'ecole."

"Didn't that, like, shut down?"

"Okay, whatever. Le Cordon Bleu."

"That's a sandwich with chicken and ham."

"Whatever, man." They both looked at Clint. "You know what I mean."

Clint shrugged. "I didn't have anything else to learn about cooking," he said, which made them laugh. "I wanted to study something else."

"So you're, like, a history major or whatever?"

"English, actually."

Goatee smiled. "Me, too," he said, holding out a hand, which Clint shook. Goatee's hands were rough, calloused, fingertips wet from dunking ping pong balls in cups of mucky water. "Seth."

"Clint."

"Nah, you're Meat Lover," Golden Eyes said.

"Okay." Clint turned to him and held out his hand. "Meat Lover."

"Jake."

They introduced him to people they knew, which seemed to be every guy and girl sitting on the ratty couches in the living room with peeling ecru paint and mismatched furniture: girls whose names immediately vanished from his memory and guys with strange nicknames like Boy Scout and Florist. Jake and Seth offered high fives to a guy they called Glacier who was manning a keg in a room that was half beer dispensary and half dance floor, music shaking the wood-paneled walls, the air filled with the odors of sweat and alcohol and body sprays. They introduced Clint to the fraternity president, who gave Clint a brief salute.

"No, man," Seth said. "This is Meat Lover!"

The president, who was stout and shaped a bit like a Lego character with nearly the same bright, almost-yellow complexion and dark eyes, squinted at Clint in the dark room, then grinned. "Holy shit. It is! Here." He handed Clint a cup of beer, even though his can of Budweiser was still half-full.

Eventually Seth disappeared, off to find a restroom, or to smoke a bowl upstairs, or something. Clint, having drank the entirety of the Budweiser and half of the cup of keg beer, was already feeling it, the edges of his vision spangly, his chest warm. That, paired with the noise of the party, made it difficult for him to hear. Jake smiled at him, sipping his own beer, and suggested they go back to the kitchen, see if the beer pong table was open.

"I've never played," Clint said.

"That's alright," Jake said, shouldering his way past bodies crammed in a hallway between rooms. "If you're as good with a ping pong ball as you are with a sirloin, you'll be fine."

For once, Clint found himself desperate to share his secret, which he'd always been happy to keep to himself. No matter the interviewer, no matter the circumstance, he never felt a yearning to reveal the source of his ability to blanch and stew. The encouraging instruction of the meats and vegetables as they guided him through proper sautéing times was something he'd always held close. But for some reason, as Jake plunged a ping pong ball into a cup of warm water he poured from a sink that was uniquely clean—the steel basin actually sparkling—he was tempted to let loose his secret despite the fact that it would make him seem crazy. He was magnetized as Jake dropped the ball into his palm, where it glistened like a gigantic pearl. Jake gestured for Clint to take a shot. Two strangers stood on the other side of the table; they hadn't introduced themselves as they arranged their cups and filled them with beer, and only now did the guy on the other side of the table nod toward Clint. The girl next to him was engrossed in her phone, only looking up when a cluster of co-eds came marching through the kitchen door.

Clint's skill at beer pong was the opposite of his prowess in front of a grill. His first half-dozen shots missed wildly, the ball bouncing off the table several inches short, or to the side, or sailing past the table entirely and into the waiting hands of his opponents. Jake seemed not to notice, making four of his own shots with ease and offering Clint nods and smiles every time the balls came their way. Thankfully, their opponents were as bad as Clint, shots arcing off the rims of the cups every time they threw. Finally, the girl made a shot, barely celebrating before returning to her phone, and Jake plucked up the cup, downing its contents. Clint watched him chug, Adam's apple bobbing, the muscles of his throat sliding with elegant length. He was struck by a sudden urge to touch Jake's neck, to feel the slip and tug of his skin. He imagined warm heat, coursing blood, easy strength. But Jake was quick to finish his drink, winking and letting out an *ahh* as he slapped the empty cup to the table.

Soon enough, Seth reappeared, and Clint was prepared to give up his space at the table, but when he said so Jake shook his head and said they were teammates now. He slapped Clint on the back and let his hand linger there for a long moment before exhorting Clint to shoot again. Clint felt a hard tremble in his teeth as he shot. For most of his teenage years, Clint had spent his time on the road, traveling across the country to various competitions, swinging through Huntsville, Alabama for The Whistlestop Wing Thing, hitting the Arizona Taco Festival, winning ten thousand dollars at the World Championship Steak Cook-off in Magnolia, Arkansas. His father homeschooled him between contests, making sure he was keeping up in mathematics and American history. Clint was smart enough, able to learn and pass all the requisite Missouri exams, scoring high on the ACT when he finally settled back into his life in St. Louis at the end of high school. But what he'd not missed educationally he had missed socially; grilling competitions were rife with middle-aged men sporting ZZ Top beards and full-sleeve tattoos and bowling shirts. They weren't the sort of people that Clint became friends with, and certainly weren't the sort for romance. When there were women around, they were brash and middle-aged, yelling at their grill assistants with raspy smokers' voices, their arms hardened with leathery muscle from so much chopping and flipping over the years. Clint never met many kids, except early on when he mashed up his fellow pre-teens in baking contests and the youth edition of *Master Chef.* And those kids were moony and weird, obsessed with cooking as an art, whereas Clint simply saw it as something he could do well to make some quick cash, which he squirreled away in his ballooning savings account.

He had to work hard not to stare at Jake, with his sharp jaw and heart-shaped face, his brow sweaty thanks to the fug and choke of bodies that had filled the kitchen. Clint's body was slick with perspiration, a combination of nerves, heat, and beer churning in his stomach. But Jake kept giving him high fives and back slaps as they played, especially on the rare occasions Clint managed to make a shot. Jake's reactions were endlessly generous, and this made Clint like him more. His teeth and lips were slimy with beer and spit, but Clint wanted to smash their mouths together, to take in Jake's breath like the scents of the kitchen. He imagined inhaling garlic and rosemary, or vanilla and apricot, salt and pepper. Maybe Jake's body would speak to him the way food did, tell him what to do, what it liked, what it wanted.

Instead, Clint felt sick.

Too much beer too fast, Jake told him later, when Clint, feeling a rapid heat strumming up his throat, let out a groan and pushed through the crowd to the door. He barely made it to the porch, rickety and old and painted a dark blue, nearly blending in with the surrounding night, before leaning over the side rail and vomiting down into the yard. A stranger smoking on the steps said, "Hell yeah, dude."

Clint felt better despite the taste in his mouth and the watering in his eyes. Jake appeared next to him, squinting down into the dark as if deeply invested in Clint's vomit.

"Puke and rally, my friend," he said. "Name of the game."

"I think I could use a break."

"Sure thing. Sit."

A bench ran the length of the rail; Clint had knelt on it as he puked. He turned and sat, the world tilting just so, his beer-addled brain working hard to calibrate. Jake sat next to him, a cup curled in his hand. He held it out toward Clint. "Here."

Clint shook his head.

"It's water. From the sink. I promise it's potable."

"Oh. Thanks."

"Just looking out."

"You don't even know me," Clint said after he drank, the water soothing the burn in his throat.

"Don't need to know someone to help them," Jake said. Then, "But I kind of do. I've watched you on TV. Lots of people in there have."

Clint shook his head. "It's all edited."

"I'm sure it is."

They sat in silence, Jake passing Clint the cup of water, Clint taking it, gulping. Jake plunged back into the party without a word, and Clint thought maybe he was gone for good, but then he came back with the same cup, freshly filled.

"Which dorm are you in?"

Clint told him, and Jake nodded. "I lived there last year before I moved into the PKG house this summer. At first I thought I'd hate the communal bathrooms, but we had a great housekeeper. She was super nice, too. Found my winter coat once and hid it in her supply closet so no one would steal it."

"That's reassuring."

"And you don't have to clean. Trust me, there will be puke in the toilets sometimes, and you won't have to be the one to deal with it."

"Good to know."

"Can I ask you something?"

"Yeah," Clint said, letting out a soft belch that made him feel immensely better.

"How'd you know you wanted to cook?"

Clint tried to think but his head felt jammed with some kind of interference, not noise exactly, but stuffing; this, he thought, was what it meant to be drunk. The truth was that he didn't really want to cook as much as he knew he could, but why not do the things you can? He'd never taken up sports because he could tell his body wasn't made for them; he didn't have the coordination to drive the lane, throw a spiral, or hit a double the way he could filet and macerate. And those things he could only do because the foods he was transforming and seasoning and butterflying told him exactly what was needed of him.

"I'm not sure," he said.

Jake nodded.

"It's just always been in my bones," Clint added, which Jake seemed to take as an acceptable answer. They fell into another silence, interrupted only by the periodic partier coming in or out, the sounds of the festivities inside a throbbing grind that spiked and fell when the door opened and closed. Jake's left leg, bare knee dusted with swirly golden hairs, was bobbing up and down, and Clint was tempted to reach out and set his hand on it.

Goateed Seth came crashing out of the party. Jake looked up and smiled. Clint wondered about the two of them.

"Dude," Seth said. "There you guys are. Some people want to meet you, Meat Lover. You've got fans!"

Clint shook his head. "I think I'm tired. I might go home?"

He saw the disappointment on Seth's face, but Clint was more concerned by Jake's muted nod.

"Oh," Seth said. "That's cool. Yeah, sure. Hey, we'll be here every night this week. Hope you come back."

Clint said thanks. He appreciated, really, that neither Seth nor Jake put up a fight, didn't try to convince him to stay and drink more.

"I think I'm heading out too," Jake said. "Wanna walk? Our house is near your dorm."

"Oh," Clint said. "Sure."

Campus was separated from the party house only by an empty parking lot and a small field of dirt and grass. Jake told him it had been occupied by a tumbledown house demolished over the summer. The fine arts building was still lit up inside, its endless wall of windows gleaming, paintings and sculptures visible from the street. Lampposts kept the sidewalks bright.

"There was an incident last year," Jake said, but offered no details.

Jake's fraternity house, it turned out, was right behind Clint's dorm, separated by a parking lot and the street.

"Now you know where to find me," Jake said, pointing. The house was a two-story, brick with white shutters, four tall columns holding up a decorative balcony above which was a trio of golden letters affixed snug beneath the pitched peak of the roof: Phi Kappa Gamma.

Clint, feeling bold, and still a little drunk despite emptying his stomach into the bushes ten minutes prior, said, "Are you hungry?"

"I could eat," Jake said.

"I mean, we could go somewhere. I'm in no shape to cook."

Jake laughed and then led him to a diner half a mile away, past the claptrap rental houses surrounding campus that gave way to the claptrap local businesses: a fuzzy antique store, a dress shop, a trophy engraver, a coffee shop advertising free Wi-Fi. Jake opened the door to a place he referred to as Shitty's, whose name was really Waffle Town. To Clint's surprise, the place was packed, a mix of drunk college students and locals, the latter hunched over a bar, several of them holding beer steins the size of pitchers. The tabletops were piss yellow, the booth seats and chairs shit brown. The harsh fluorescent light made Jake look sallow, his drunkenness more obvious in the liquid of his eyes and the red of his cheeks.

Jake told Clint he had to order the Lumberjack Platter on his first visit—"It's tradition"—and so he did, asking for a glass of water from their waitress, who looked harried and tired, her teal polo shirt and khaki pants smeared with syrup and ranch dressing. Jake asked for a basket of cheese curds, which he told Clint, once the waitress was gone, was the one thing on the menu that was legitimately delicious.

"I mean," he said, "it's all good when you're hammered." He leaned in. "You could cook the snot out of anything, I bet."

All Clint could think to do was nod and drink, the icy water cool and soothing on his still-burning throat. He sat back in the booth and felt a sudden exhaustion.

"I'm guessing you judge food a lot when you go out to eat."

"Oh," Clint said. "Not really."

"I probably would, if I was as good as you. I'd probably never be happy with a meal someone else made."

"My parents are good cooks."

"So maybe they inspired you."

"They're not that good."

This made Jake snort. Clint wondered, again, if he should tell him the truth. If he could tell him the truth. Would Jake, this stranger who was becoming more than that, believe him, or would he think that Clint was insane, or just drunk, or, worse, some kind of jerk making a bad joke?

Their food arrived before he had to decide, Jake's cheese curds golden and bright in their red basket with butcher paper lining. Clint's meal took up three obscenely large plates, one of them stacked with four pancakes, another with two slices of ham and a spray of hash browns that smelled of black pepper, the third home to two over-easy eggs and a pair of sausage links and four triangles of wheat toast.

"Whoa," he said.

"Dig in."

Clint ate. The sausage was the slippery, squeaky kind, smooth tubes of meat that had been over-processed to a textureless mass given flavor only by a hearty shake of pepper. The eggs were almost vulcanized, but the ham was juicy. Clint nodded as he took bites of toast; after each bite, he felt hungrier, his drunken body glad for the grease and calories. Jake tossed cheese curds in his mouth as if he was eating popcorn. Maybe, Clint thought, watching him wolf down food was, for Jake, like a night at the movies.

When Clint took a break—he hadn't even started on the pancakes—Jake held up a cheese curd. "Try one of these."

He leaned over the table, arm outstretched, cheese curd beckoning like a plucked grape held by an attendant. Clint opened his mouth and Jake dropped the curd in, but his fingers lingered at Clint's lips. He didn't know what to do, and he wished that the bacon and hash browns would speak, guide him. Clint blinked, then slowly closed his mouth, giving Jake enough time to withdraw his fingers.

When they were finished eating, Clint felt bloated and a little sick. The smells wafting from the kitchen—burning meat, overcooked eggs, toast smoking to black—made his stomach flop. Jake paid, despite Clint's objections.

"It was my idea, so it's my treat."

"Wasn't it my idea?"

Jake smiled and shrugged. "I don't remember it that way."

"My food cost way more."

Jake snorted. "Nothing costs 'way more' here. Even the T-bone steak is, like, nine dollars."

Clint noticed that Jake left a massive tip, a ten dollar bill he tucked under his depleted water glass, and this warmed Clint's cheeks. His mother had been a waitress all through college; she'd taught him to be generous in restaurants, regardless of the quality of service.

"You never know what they're going through," she had said more than once. "Maybe they're having a bad day. Maybe whatever went wrong isn't their fault."

Somehow, the air was heavier and hotter when they left the diner, a weighted blanket pushing on Clint's shoulders. Warm wind swiveled down the street, pulling the smell of fresh tar along with it. A cluster of students passed them on the sidewalk, two of them greeting Jake and offering high fives.

"You know a lot of people," Clint said.

"You will, too. It's that kind of school."

"That's nice."

"I guess. It's the kind of knowing where you know people's names, but you don't really know them. It's hard to know people here."

"What about Seth?"

Jake laughed. "What about him?"

"You guys seem close."

Jake nodded. "Well, yeah. We're friends, but. You know." He shrugged, a tilted smile working at the edges of his lips. "There are always things people don't know."

"Like what?"

"I dunno. The kind of things you never tell people, I guess."

They'd reached an intersection: turn left to go to Jake's fraternity house, or go straight to hit Clint's dorm.

"Food speaks to me," Clint said. "That's how I'm so good. At cooking. It tells me what it wants."

"That sure would help, huh?" Jake said. "Easier when things tell you exactly what to do."

"Yes," Clint said. Jake's gaze had gone vacant, distant, like he was peering at something on the far horizon. Clint could tell Jake had misunderstood. He swallowed a dry breath; despite drinking four glasses of water at the diner, he could feel the hard ridges of his palate. His tongue was like a beefsteak, clunky and dry and uncontrollable. "It is."

Jake looked at him and let out a low sigh, a long-held breath. His shoulders rolled forward, and he reached up a hand to rub at one of his eyes. He smiled. "Well, Meat Lover."

"Yeah?"

"This was fun."

The air was dead around them. Clint could only nod. They stared at one another for a long, silent moment, and then the bubbling noise of a group of drunk students wandering up the street broke the quiet. Clint stared at them, the girls in their short-shorts, the guys in jeans or khaki shorts, all of their legs golden with summer sun. They were slumped together, bodies braided, arms across shoulders in intimate entanglement. Jake gave them a glance and then looked back at Clint. He blinked and smiled, his grin lopsided. Clint tried to smile, too, but he couldn't bring himself to do so. He mumbled a quiet goodbye, then turned away, not letting himself look back. As he crossed the lot, he thought he heard something, a whispered call, but perhaps it was just the wind. Or maybe it was the cluster of partiers on their way to a new destination. Maybe it was Jake, calling for him to come back. Or maybe it was any of the millions of other living things that surrounded him, preparing to tell him what to do next.

Mariah

Alan's roommates were the kind of assholes who, instead of sneaking into the bathroom while he showered and dumping a bucket of cold ice water over the curtain, broke in and recorded him singing along to "Always Be My Baby," of which, in Alan's estimation, he hit every note. Alan's roommates were the kind of assholes who shared said video with the rest of his fraternity brothers after the next PKG chapter meeting. They were the kind of assholes who tried to get everyone to start calling him Mariah because, despite their best efforts to make other nicknames stick, none of them had. Alan wasn't a fucking moron like the rest of his friends who kept doing the same stupid shit every weekend when they were hammered on Natural Light and their IQs descended to those of sloths. Unlike his friends and dipshit roommates, he knew how to not black out before ten-thirty. He knew how to not piss himself, unlike P-Stain, and he knew how to not smash his head into walls, unlike Concussion, and he definitely knew how to not get behind the wheel of his car and end up lost on one of the state highways that unfurled out past their small college town into the boonies, unlike DD.

What Alan did know was most of Mariah Carey's discography. And not just the popular stuff. Anyone could hum along to "We Belong Together" and "Hero" and, of course, "All I Want For Christmas Is You." But Alan had long memorized tracks off *Glitter* and *The Emancipation of Mimi*; he could karaoke "After Tonight" and "Petals," even if they weren't on offer, nailing the lyrics to perfection. He couldn't always hit the inhuman high notes, but he had a good ear for pitch, and when he needed to knock things down an octave, he knew when and where to do it.

He wasn't a psycho fan; he didn't know Mariah Carey's birthday, or her kids' names, or where she lived. Alan hadn't even been to a concert. His older sister had been the one steeped in Mariah's life and music, blasting *Charmbracelet* all through high school, which she called an underappreciated masterpiece that critics simply didn't understand. Carolyn was the worse singer of the two of them, unable to carry a tune or sing above middle-C without sounding like a razzy radio, and so she spent her time lip-syncing, bopping around her bedroom with abandon even when she knew Alan was standing in the doorway watching. Instead of mocking her, he would tap his foot along to the beat and, eventually, start singing. At the time he was too young to understand how people might mock him for this, and his sister didn't disabuse him. She invited him into her room and stopped jumping on her bed and fake-singing into the blow dryer, eyes wide with admiration and a bit of jealousy as she listened.

His asshole roommates didn't comment on Alan's skill. They passed around the video, hunched in threes and fours over cell phones, squinting at the shaky footage of the bland, cream-colored bathroom with matching shower curtain and off-white vanity. Ambient noise and the fuzzy breathing of the hungover cinematographer washed out Alan's voice.

"He can sing," they said.

DD was the first to actually call him Mariah, three days after the video's initial circulation. He and Alan were standing on opposite sides of the beer pong table erected in the main foyer of the PKG house, where people congregated on the weekends to drink shitty beer and do shots out of glasses emblazoned with their fraternity crest, which looked like a medieval jousting shield, a trio of stars at the top, and their letters—Phi Kappa Gamma—etched along the lower edge. The table was actually a lacquered plywood construction sign painted blue and white with a company logo, stolen a few years prior when the dorm across the street was being renovated. It was good for pong, as it didn't absorb sloshed beer or sprays of water from the rinsing cup that everyone knew was doing jack squat to prevent contamination after the ball rolled across the floor and sometimes skittered into the men's bathroom.

DD shouted it out when Alan was lining up a shot at the final cup he and his teammate Simon needed to make to win the game. Alan had been having a good night, sinking cup after cup, he and his partner racking up six wins on the trot, dismissing challengers in quick fashion. Before each of his shots, Alan hummed a few bars of "I'll Be There" to relax and focus and—bam, splash—down went the ping pong ball with a small plume of beer foam.

"Did he just call you Mariah?" Simon said after Alan shot and missed, the ball clipping the cup's back inner lip and glancing off to the side.

Alan nodded. Simon was a quiet tow-haired boy a year younger than him. People called him Cherub because of the flaxen, near-white of his hair and the way his cheeks went deeply ruddy when he drank or was embarrassed, which happened a lot when he drank. He and Alan had hooked up a few times the year prior, awkward attempts at mutual pleasure. They sorted out, the first time, that neither had even a remotely passing interest in anal sex, which seemed especially challenging to plan for unless one wanted a horribly messy affair, which Alan had noted aloud, making Simon snort. So far, two months into the school year, he and Simon had picked up their casual affability where it had left off at the start of summer but hadn't yet fallen back into bed together.

"Is it because you can sing?" Simon asked after DD tried out the nickname. Simon was a bit of a lightweight, and with enough beer his voice went child-like, as did the whimsy of his questions. This entertained Alan, far more than the pranks and insulting stupidity of DD, P-Stain, and Concussion. There had been a period when, the first few times he and Simon had gnashed at one another, he was worried about what his roommates might say or do should they find out (Simon, still living in the dorm, had shacked up in Alan's room in his apartment, slinking out early enough that the Neanderthals were still snoring off their hangovers). They did find out, somehow, even though Simon claimed not to have said a word; perhaps one of them caught sight of Simon's golden head as he tumbled down the stairs from their porch, or watched him skitter across the street heading back toward campus, and put everything together. They made periodic comments while playing vintage Super Mario Brothers on their Nintendo Wii, asking after Simon with only the slightest wryness in their voices, but that was it. No nickname. Alan had imagined something like Cradle Robber or Baby Snatcher. But he got nothing.

"It is," Alan said, catching DD's shot after it came up short, bouncing in front of and skimming over the cups. "You haven't seen the video?"

"Yes, I have," Simon said. "You're good."

Alan's face felt hot. Something else that happened when Simon was drunk was that he got all lovey-dovey. Sometimes at chapter meetings, Alan would feel a weird tingle on the back of his neck and he'd look around, find Simon perched on the basement's bar top or standing in the back, leaning on the cement wall, looking his way. Every time, Simon kept looking, a little smile on his face. Or sometimes he'd wave, as if Alan was a passing beauty queen on a parade float and Simon an adoring onlooker.

Alan managed to sink his next shot, catching DD off-guard as he chatted with the girl he'd recruited to be his partner, probably hoping to hook up with her after they lost and wandered away from the table. Simon offered Alan a celebratory high five, his hand clammy and slick from dunking the ping pong balls over and over in their water cup.

Simon asked if Alan would play another game and he nodded yes. Why not? The party was a dud, only twenty people or so scattered about the foyer despite it being Friday night. He watched DD and the girl he'd played with slink out the front door as Concussion and P-Stain slid up to the table, asking if anyone had next game. They looked like they'd been pulled out of a fishing magazine, each wearing a ridiculous bucket hat and short-sleeved button-down shirt left open to reveal white undershirts stained with beer— or what Alan hoped was beer but could have easily been the vestiges of vomit, knowing his moronic cohabitants. As soon as the game started, both of them started humming "Thank God I Found You" every time Alan aimed at the cups, trying to match his tune.

He switched to some lesser-known tracks, lowering his voice. But somehow they followed along.

"Did you dick holes study or something?"

"Definitely not the 'or something,'" Concussion said, grinning. His mouth was purled with saliva, little white gloms at the edges, and his shots were terrible, half of them missing the table entirely. He hit Simon square in the chest with a missile of a throw.

Despite how awful their opponents were, Alan was thrown off by the skull fuckery of his roommates, who were swaying like they were on a bucking ship. He kept missing, and badly, his shots hitchy, as though something was popping and grinding in his elbow. His fingers throbbed. Simon kept them afloat, making three shots in a row at one point, but soon enough they were facing down a four-cup deficit, with P-Stain shooting at one remaining cup to take them out. He missed and staggered, nearly catapulting himself into his own cups.

"Come on Mariah," Concussion said, helping P-Stain steady himself. His voice rose to a falsetto. "You can make it, baby."

"Pretty sure that's not a Mariah line," Simon said.

"Oh, can it, Angel Face," Concussion said.

"Dude," Alan said, shaking his head. "What is your problem?"

P-Stain just shook his head, looking like he needed to vomit.

Alan whispered himself a line from "Heartbreaker" and shot, knowing, as soon as he let go, that it would go in. It splashed into one of the cups, and Simon quickly took his turn, sinking a cup as well. He offered Alan a high five.

"Fags," Concussion muttered.

The party didn't stop; there was no screeching halt to the music, no appalled staring. Alan wasn't even sure if anyone else had heard. He wasn't sure Concussion even knew what he'd said, be-

cause he rolled the balls across the table and kept swaying as normal. But Alan felt a blast of heat in his face; his feet were concret-
ed to the floor. Of course he'd heard that word before, but never
directed his way. P-Stain, his face grizzled with days-old scruff,
didn't appear to have heard his teammate, and neither did Simon.
Alan imagined he was going slowly insane. Perhaps he could be
given some nickname for that, Cuckoo Clock or Schizo or Here's
Johnny or whatever.

Simon was quick to shoot, sinking another cup, which looked
as if it caused P-Stain physical pain. He plucked the cup up, ex-
tracted the ball, and drank, fast, letting out a wet belch that Alan
could practically smell from across the table. A girl nearby hooted
in drunk admiration and disgust, and P-Stain saluted her with a
cheers of his empty cup. Concussion was staring at Alan, who
could just about hear his thoughts. He saw that Concussion's eyes
were on his lips, just waiting for him to whisper his mantra.

Instead he shot right away. And he missed.

"Three out of four ain't bad," Simon said, and Concussion
rolled his eyes.

Alan wanted to ask, again, what the fuck his problem was.
Concussion might be a drunken idiot, but he wasn't a complete
asshole, the video aside, which Alan had already convinced himself had been driven by good fun and stupid college bro jocularity.
But something else was happening, clearly, as if Concussion had
rotted from the inside out overnight. His eyes were daggered in
Alan's direction as he shot, not even bothering to look toward the
cups, so of course he missed, wildly, letting out a roar of frustra-
tion and punching his fist down on the edge of the table, sloshing
the liquid in the remaining cups, sending Alan and Simon's final
target sliding across the slippery surface.

"Can we get a retouch?" Simon said.

"Oh, fuck off, Angel Face," Concussion said. P-Stain blinked at him but reset the cup before taking his own shot, which banked off the edge of the table and into the bathroom. Alan went to retrieve it, so he didn't hear or see whatever happened next, not until there came a loud crash. When he turned and looked, Simon was on the ground, shoved up against the wall. Where the party had not been stanched into surprised silence by Concussion's previous bigoted outburst, it was now, all eyes staring toward Simon, who had a dazed look on his face. Concussion was looming not directly over him but near enough that Alan could tell he was the culprit. The table was slanted to the side as if hip-checked, and the cup that P-Stain and Concussion had been failing to make had been knocked over, beer dribbling over the side like a pathetic waterfall. Alan gripped the ball in his hand.

"What the fuck is going on?" he said, stepping out of the bathroom.

"Your chode-lick partner called me a homo."

"Fairy," Simon croaked, feeling at the back of his head. "I called him a fairy."

"Fuck you."

"Hey," Alan said. "What is wrong with you?"

Concussion looked from Alan to Simon and back, then twisted to glance at the faces staring in his direction. P-Stain, for all his own stupidity, was standing, shell-shocked, on the other side of the table, hands buried in his jeans pockets, eyes downward as if to try to deny any association. Alan could feel the hot glare of a dozen sets of eyes as he knelt next to Simon, ignoring Concussion as he started to stammer and sway and then trundled out of the party, elbowing his way through a congested bundle of people, jostling several girls and causing a wave of spilled drinks.

"Are you okay?" Alan said.

Simon's eyes were large. Alan had no idea if this was from being drunk or in shock or having a concussion of his own. But he managed to focus on Alan and his mouth curled into a woozy smile.

"I called him a fairy, Alan."

"You did. Let's get you upstairs, if you can walk."

"Sure thing."

Alan hauled Simon to his feet, Simon gripping him at the elbow. Alan remembered the feeling of Simon's fingers, how, despite the willowy look of his arms, not helped by the baby-boy look of his face, he had a strong grip, years of teenaged rock climbing. Even once Simon was steady on his feet, he didn't let go of Alan, and they walked to the staircase with Simon slumped against him. Before they went upstairs, Alan turned and waved goodbye to some PKGs in the corner of the room; Simon, arm flapping, did the same.

The PKG house was large but hardly a mansion; none of the fraternity houses on their corn-fed Midwestern campus were. The carpet leading upstairs was a washed-out cerulean that reminded Alan of putting greens and 1970s basements, and it scratched under Simon's shuffling feet as they turned at the midpoint landing and made for the upper floor. The walls were scuffed white, years of drunk stumbling and fisticuffs leaving divots in the drywall and streaks of muted color through the paint.

Upstairs, Alan fished out his keys; the door at the upper landing was locked during parties so random strangers didn't wander through the members' rooms. The hallway was horseshoe-shaped, curling around a pair of rooms with no exterior windows they called The Caskets, their lack of sunshine offset by the Jack-and-Jill private bathroom the four PKGs who lived there were afforded; this allowed them to avoid the communal one with its overflowing trashcan and scuzzy vanities that barely ever received a good scrubbing.

"Which room is yours?" Alan said.

"You've sucked my dick and don't know where I live?" Simon said.

"Jesus, Simon." Alan looked around: the second floor was empty, unless the handful of cracked doors with dark interiors held PKGs lying in wait for juicy gossip.

"Sorry," Simon said. "But it's true." His voice trilled to a high pitch and Simon giggled, then told Alan he was in the corner room, before the turn, a three-person unit with a pair of closets that didn't have doors. The walls were the same rich navy blue as the others and were covered in PKG paraphernalia: hand towels and t-shirts thumb-tacked to the walls, along with a pair of wooden paddles—purely decorative, as Alan had been assured when he was a fresh-man going on a tour of the house—and several old posters for rush weeks gone by. The room was largely clean, a pair of bunked beds with fresh sheets carefully arrayed, plus a solo bed, which turned out to be Simon's, with sheets twisted and pillows askew. Out of one closet spilled a heap of dirty laundry that let off a musty smell. Alan deposited Simon on his bed.

"Do you want some water, Simon?"

"That'd be nice, yes."

Alan found a drinking glass on one of the small desks crammed in a neat row that looked clean enough. In the bathroom, he avoided the crusty cans of Barbasol and crinkled toothpaste tubes that were gathered around the sinks like sentries. He filled the glass, ignoring the slightly-occluded coloring. When he came back to the room, Simon was lying down, staring at the ceiling.

"You should probably sit up, Simon. Until we know you're okay."

"You're the only one, Alan."

"Excuse me?" He held out the water but Simon didn't take it.

"Everyone else calls me Cherub. Only you call me Simon." His hands were on his stomach, near his belt, fingers prying at the hem of his shirt. Alan swallowed a hard breath, imagining that Simon might start undressing. The sight of his hands made a quiver wash over the back of his neck and down his throat. He remembered the sight lines of Simon's body, how his skin had the shine of a varnished pearl, smooth and blank and pristine aside from a thatch of well-kempt pubic hair that matched that on his head. His scrotum was dusted with a soft pelt of it, and touching Simon there, feeling the skin contract beneath his fingers and mouth, had been like coming into contact with a docile animal.

"Simon is your name. Why would I call you anything else?"

Simon shook his head but smiled. "It's my nickname."

"Nicknames are stupid."

"Are you saying I'm not cherubic?"

"No, Simon."

Simon sat up, wobbling. "Good. You shouldn't. I need to tell you something."

Alan was still holding the water glass, which had gone slick in his hand. Simon took it, finally, and drank with a swift urgency, the knob of his Adam's apple bouncing. His throat was swan-like, long and elegant. Alan remembered biting into it just so, as if he were about to eat a pillowy slice of cake; the pressure of his teeth had made Simon groan, the noise vibrating through Alan's entire body.

Simon finished drinking and gave Alan the glass. "I hooked up with Concussion this summer."

"What?" Alan said. He stared at the glass, the surface smeary with fingerprints. His heart was beating too fast.

"We were both in Kansas City. We hung out one night. He got too drunk, so he stayed at my house. He stumbled into my room and, well, things happened."

"Oh." Alan tried to picture his asshole roommate kissing Simon and he couldn't. He couldn't imagine anyone else peeling away Simon's underwear, tongue exploring the tender spot between thigh and testicles the way Alan knew made him go wild.

"He wanted me," Simon said in a conspiratorial whisper, "to stick my finger in his asshole."

Alan suddenly felt very drunk. He could still see Concussion standing over Simon's slumped form, fists curled tight, fingernails digging into the soft peachy skin of his palms. The word *fag* whispered out in a dark, grim rasp. How Concussion's day-old stubble reminded Alan of gangrene. How sometimes, when it was just the two of them in their apartment, Concussion might start jawing with a flamboyant, sissy voice, making fun of whoever was the least masculine character in whatever movie or television show they were watching.

"Did you?" Alan said.

"Did I what?"

"Stick your finger in his asshole."

Simon laughed. He stared at Alan and slowly nodded. "He wanted me to do more than that, too."

Alan's mouth was dry. He stared down at the smudged, empty glass. "And did you?"

"I did." Simon's voice was low.

"Oh."

"I thought we were over, Alan."

"We were, I guess."

Alan hadn't so much as kissed anyone else in the months since. The summer had been hot and dry and uninviting, and he'd barely gone out, even though he'd turned twenty-one and suddenly the worlds of Soulard, the Central West End, and The Landing were available to him. He could have had a raucous summer, sleeping with any number of strangers, but he'd not found the energy or motivation. Now he had a headache, and he didn't know what to say, to do. He could only picture Simon and Concussion, bodies thrusting into one another. Nausea and heat welled in his throat.

"I'm not, like, in love with him," Simon said. "He didn't want anyone to know."

Alan wasn't sure what to say. He kept staring down at the glass, remembering all the times Simon had slunk out of his apartment the year prior. All the times they'd gone to parties, behaving as if nothing was going on, Alan tingling with the knowledge that they would probably be touching and tugging at one another in only a few hours.

Simon sat up and put an arm around Alan. His breath was close, sweet and sour with beer and spittle. After so long without the touch of another person so close, Alan felt a wash of pleasure at the simpleness of human contact.

"Will you sing to me?" Simon whispered, voice close, breath on Alan's ear.

"What?"

"Sing to me."

"Simon."

"Call me Cherub. Everyone calls me Cherub."

"I don't want to."

"One or the other. Singing or Cherub."

Once, when he was singing with his sister, Alan's father had barged into the room without knocking. Carolyn screamed about privacy, but when she saw the look on his face, she shut her mouth. He was staring at Alan, who'd cocked out a hip and let out a trilled high noise. He, too, froze, and stared at his father, whose bearded face was a series of hard lines. Even as a kid, he knew that he'd inherited his mother's delicate features instead of his dad's rugged manliness. He stood straight, knees locked, wondering what his father would do.

"You sound good," his dad said, then backed out of the room, closing the door. He and Carolyn stared at one another while the song, "My All," came to its close.

Alan set down the glass and leaned into Simon's weight. He felt a hard pain in his stomach, as if someone had reached in and twisted his intestines. Simon's body shifted back toward the mattress, but he didn't lie down. Alan was tempted to push him over, to climb atop him, kiss him hard, ravage him. But the look on Simon's face was serene, his eyes closed, lips purled into an angelic smile. Alan took a long breath. He wouldn't refer to Simon as Cherub—never. So instead he skimmed through the songs he knew, plucked out "Obsessed," and began to sing. But Simon raised a finger to Alan's lips and shook his head.

"No, no. You're not Mariah, remember? You're Alan."

"So?"

"Sing me your song."

"I don't have a song."

Simon shrugged. "Make something up."

At first, Alan didn't think he could. He didn't have words, but he opened his mouth and sound came out—non-language, a deep, throbbing hum. Simon put his hand to Alan's chest, which seemed to open his throat, the noise louder. Simon nodded. Alan felt warmth throughout his body. He felt the vibration of his body deep inside, and he let words form, new, never before spoken, and started to sing.

Goodnight Guys

People laughed when they were told they couldn't leave without saying bye to the Goodnight Guys, until they tried to open the Phi Kappa Gamma fraternity house's front door and the knob wouldn't turn. Or, if the door was propped open, as was often the case because the air conditioning was constantly on the fritz, they would march toward the entryway and stop all of a sudden, as if they'd run splat into an invisible wall. Their eyes would go wide and they would look around, sweaty and drunk, until someone pointed out Daniil and Davis, the twins who were usually wearing sleeveless shirts and sunglasses, eternally partnered up for beer pong, at which they were unnaturally good and often went undefeated. They would quit when one of them—usually Daniil—eventually passed out against the trophy case, which boasted PKG's many awards for being good at indoor volleyball and winning the university's annual Homecoming lip sync competition, and had to be hoisted up by the other.

They were mirror twins, discernible from one another only because Daniil had a Cindy Crawford mole on the left side of his face where Davis' was on his right. They looked otherwise the same, with the same jet-black hair cut high and tight, the same dimples, the same lean, muscular frames, the same skin that went reddish-gold after a day in the sun. Daniil was an English major, Davis, economics, but Daniil was an econ minor and Davis took creative writing classes for fun, so they were just about equally versed in Walter Benjamin and Nathaniel Hawthorne. They shared a room on the second floor, with matching bedspreads on their matching lofted beds, beneath which were identical IKEA desks. They'd pledged the same semester, and they both had the same tattoo stenciled in slanted back letters on their forearms, Daniil's on his left, Davis' on his right: the first sentence of *One Hundred Years of Solitude*, their favorite book. They were idiots when they were drunk, the Cardinals baseball caps they wore riding higher and higher on their heads, their voices slurred and spit-addled, shoulders slumped, but when they were sober, they were the smartest guys in the house, each with a perfect GPA.

No one quite knew when they became the Goodnight Guys, or how or why they'd cast—purposefully or otherwise—the spell that hovered over the PKG house. As with so many booze-stained traditions, the fact of having to say goodbye to them seemed to have sprung out of nowhere. But people who marched into the PKG house knew that if they wanted to march out they had to offer a goodbye hug or high five or a called out "See ya!" from across the room if the Goodnight Guys were partying. They understood that they could go outside without saying a word, but only if their intention was to smoke a cigarette or get some air, to enjoy the cool quiet of crisp October or the woodsmoke of a fire glowing in the pit out back. Or even to puke or take a piss along the fence line that the property shared with the bitch of a philosophy professor who was constantly complaining of the noise, even on Saturday afternoons when all they were doing was barbecuing and casually drinking Bud Selects. If, however, anyone tried to leave the property after such sojourns, their feet would turn to lead, bodies unable to galumph off the grass or into the parking lot, and they would have to march inside, find one of the Goodnight Guys, and say adieu.

For nearly two years people laughed about it, nervous at first when their feet wouldn't whisk them out the door, when the doorknobs wouldn't turn in their clenched fists, but otherwise ultimately unharmed. But on a late-March Saturday night, the house was jammed with people, the air like a jungle, piqued with sweat and spittle and beer, and someone threw open all the windows, the noise of the party spilling out into the night, and the cops appeared, knocking on the front door. All the minors freaked out, dropped their drinks, and tried to funnel themselves out the back while the fraternity president handled the police, accepting the noise complaint ticket with solemn apology. But the door wouldn't budge. Bodies pressed against one another, and one girl shrieked that she was being felt up. Then another did the same. Soon a cacophony had erupted, and someone screamed out for the Goodnight Guys, who were slumped on a couch, passing a pint of Southern Comfort back and forth. Someone eventually got their attention, and they started waving and calling out goodbyes, and finally the crowd of undergraduates was set free. By then, though, the police were ready for them, grabbing up students as soon as they left the property, handing out MIPs to partiers stupid enough to slink off with beers in their pockets or airline bottles of Smirnoff in their purses.

Something, the PKGs agreed the next day as they grumbled through their hangovers and worried about potential consequences for the fiasco, had to be done about the Goodnight Guys.

Φ Κ Γ

The science-minded PKGs tried experiments: what about off-campus party houses, where the Goodnight Guys were guests? What about the bars on the downtown square, where the drinks were cheap and watered-down? What about when the Goodnight Guys went home for Labor Day weekend or Thanksgiving, or were in the Gulf Shores during spring break? All of those were safe: people could come and go, worried not at all about their ability to sneak out. And if the Goodnight Guys went to bed early? What might happen then? It took a lot to keep the Goodnight Guys away from a party; in fact, in order to find out whether people could leave if the guys were snug in their beds on the second floor, the fraternity president offered each of them one hundred of his own dollars if they would spend a Friday night cooped up in their room while people danced and chugged beer and played Up and Down the River, their bedroom walls rattling from the heavy bass of the rap music pumping out of the stereo system. The Goodnight Guys agreed, and, lo and behold, people were able to walk out of the house without saying goodbye to a single soul.

And what if they were separated? What if Daniil was conked out, head resting on his Serta pillow while Davis entertained his friends and flirted with the guy from his macroeconomics class he'd invited over? Or if Davis was out like a light while Daniil fist-bumped a stranger when he sank a cup, giving them the balls back in beer pong? Another offering was made, this time from the fraternity's general fund, and Davis spent a lonely Friday slumped at his desk, watching Netflix while his brother slammed Keystone. That night, the doorknob turned with a silky immediacy, the doorway freely passable.

But people left that party feeling off, as if they shouldn't have stumbled into the night or a sober driver's car. They woke up the next day itchy for another bout of heavy drinking and spastic dancing, and the house was packed with bodies hours before the usual eleven-at-night rush. Daniil took his turn sequestered upstairs while the music and booze flowed into the basement, a raucous party where someone unfolded the humongous inflatable waterslide shaped like a castle that the fraternity kept in their storage shed for rush week. The police were eventually called by unhappy neighbors trying to get a good night's sleep, and the partygoers slumped away, disconsolate and again filled with that inexplicable itch. Daniil watched, sober, from his bedroom window as clusters of co-eds carried their cases of beer off into the night. No one had to say goodbye to Davis, who walked in and leaned against the bedroom door, eyes glossy with light beer, and said, "Missed you, bro."

Daniil turned to his brother. "Missed you, too."

At Sunday's chapter meeting, held in the damp, warm basement, the fluorescent lights revealed the dark circles under people's eyes.

"We can't have people unable to leave," the president said.

"Right," the Vice President said. "It's a risk management hazard. What if there was a fire?"

"We'd be screaming goodbyes," Daniil said.

"We'd probably have high-tailed it out ourselves," Davis said. His voice was scratchy and raw.

"Still," the president said. "It's freaking people out."

"Who is it freaking out?" Davis asked, arms crossed. Sober, he and his brother were ready to launch into a sophisticated self-defense. They watched their fellow PKGs shift in their seats. "Who here is freaked out?"

No one answered or looked him in the eye. Davis slapped his thighs with his hands. "Cowards," he said. "What are you going to do? Demand one of us skip every party? We pay dues, too, you know."

"And we both felt what you all felt after," Daniil said. "Don't pretend you don't wish there was a party tonight."

The others could do nothing but nod. Instead of listening to the treasurer's report, or caring about who was scheduled to sober drive next week, or how planning for spring formal was going, they all wanted to throw a party. Rare, unusual, Sundays were the one night that most everyone was quieted up in their rooms by ten, studying or playing video games, drinking bottles of Mountain Dew and munching on potato chips instead of taking shots of Popov and slamming Steele Reserve. But they all knew what Daniil was referring to: that itchy desire, a need to mill with a drink in hand, to play card games and dance without reservation, to find someone to make out with in one of the house's dark corners, to wake up in the morning with a dry mouth and a dizzied stomach. To have said goodbye to the Goodnight Guys before marching off into the dark.

Φ Κ Γ

No party came, but neither did any changes. The PKGs argued back and forth, Davis and Daniil parrying every thrust with complicated language and references to authors—DeLillo, Poe, Ann Beatty—and economists—Keynes, Smith, Maynard, even Marx— mostly because the names confused and bewildered their hungover brethren. The Goodnight Guys wore their peers down with their oratory, and eventually the president said, "Okay, okay, whatever," and the next weekend the Goodnight Guys were back where they belonged, dominating at beer pong from their usual end of the table, backlit by the trophy case and its wares. Daniil had just gotten back a major essay in his Shakespeare course, receiving an A for his examination of the influence of "The Dream of the Rood" on the history plays, and Davis had scored the highest grade on the midterm in his Time Series Econometrics class. They'd busted out a fifth of cheap gin, taking shots every ten minutes, polishing off the bottle before ten. Their cheeks were identically red, the skin around their mirrored moles inflamed scarlet, and they wore their ubiquitous sunglasses and baseball caps. When they belched, the air filled with the Chinese food they'd scarfed at the one decent buffet in town, where the crab rangoon was made spicy with curry and where the waitresses were so fast at refilling your water glass that it was an unspoken competition to see who could manage to drink it down to just ice cubes before one of them showed up with a pitcher to top you off.

Davis and Daniil kept winning, teetering up to the edge of the beer pong table to make their shots, vision focusing long enough for them to plunk the balls right into the foam crowning their opponents' cups. They took on all comers, and they accepted cries of departure with grumbled responses and waves of dismissal. As midnight passed and the Goodnight Guys won their sixth game in a row by more than five cups, a weird pallor fell over the house, the grim anger in Davis and Daniil's throws spreading like infection. People who had been dancing with freedom and joy found themselves stomping to rap music, anger thrumming through their heels, their fists raised in clenches of inexplicable protest. Conversations turned to irritated arguments about inane things like which professional sport required more talent, or whether it was normal to wear t-shirts sporting a university one didn't attend.

Later, no one would be quite sure who had started the scuffle between the Goodnight Guys and the president, a short, stocky junior with swimmer's shoulders who took himself too seriously to be particularly fun but who handled himself well at Interfraternity Council meetings and also knew how to hold his own when alumni showed up looking to do things that violated their bylaws. He was a bio major who spent hours at the library, and everyone knew that he shook his head privately at the way the Goodnight Guys could get drunk all the time and still maintain sterling grades. He worked hard, and he rarely got so blasted that he stumbled or slurred, usually hanging out on the periphery of parties while nursing a craft beer. But that night, he was in a state. Someone had been plying him with Captain Morgan, his weakness; it was the one thing that he drank and kept on drinking. Right before Davis was about to take aim at the last cup the Goodnight Guys needed to make in their seventh game, he approached them, emerging from the bathroom.

Some people said that the president grumbled about wanting to go to bed. Others said that he hissed an insult toward the brothers. Still more thought he didn't say anything at all, though it was clear that something passed between him and the Goodnight Guys because everyone heard Daniil say, "Well, go to fucking bed, then," and pointed toward the stairs. The president stood there and shook his head, and then, out of nowhere, started screaming, "Goodnight, goodnight, goodnight!" Davis grinned in response. And then the president said, "You guys think you're so fucking special."

"Well, I don't see people saying goodnight to you," Daniil said, poking the president in the chest. Those close by thought it was just a quick, light jab. Others would claim that Daniil shoved the president, hard enough for him to stumble backward so that he bumped up against the trophy case. Whatever happened, the president then stepped toward Daniil, one shoulder lowered like he was going in for a tackle. Davis stepped in from the side and pushed the president, and this time the intention was undeniable. The president reeled backward, clipped the side of the trophy case, and fell to the floor. Someone turned off the music. Drinks hovered at lips, in hands. Dancers stopped moving as if frozen in time. The president, lying on his stomach, let out a groan and started to push himself up, then splayed on the ground.

The Goodnight Guys stared down at him. Later they would say they could see he was breathing, his eyes open and roving, his lips pressed firm into a frown. They would claim the president was milking things, feigning injury for the sake of victimhood. The president, when he wrote up a formal complaint against both of the Goodnight Guys and submitted it to the vice president, requested that the twins be kicked out of the fraternity. He claimed he thought he'd suffered a concussion, even though he never went to the hospital or the campus health center and woke up the next morning complaining only of a stomach ache from drinking too much rum.

One of the sober drivers helped the president get to his feet and led him upstairs to his bedroom, where the sober driver fed him a handful of ibuprofen and two glasses of water. The party eventually came back to life, the music slowly turned back up to its wall-grinding volume, the dancers unfreezing, their bodies finding the beat. Those playing card games figured out whose turn it had been, and conversations picked up where they'd paused. The Goodnight Guys tried to finish their game of beer pong, but neither of them found themselves caring. They lost, despite a sizable lead, and they shrugged at one another when they gave up their place at the table.

They slunk upstairs to their shared room but they didn't go to bed. Daniil stood before the window while Davis sat at his desk, staring at the dark screen of his laptop. Neither spoke. The sounds of the party wafted up through the floor boards and air vent, a conglomeration of buzzy music, laughter, and voices. Daniil looked down at the empty lawn.

"They don't appreciate us," he said. "What if we just stopped going to parties? Would anyone even notice?"

Davis was looking at himself in the dark laptop screen. He peeled off his sunglasses. It struck him that he was tired, and drunk, and also only had until Monday to complete a short story for his writing class that he'd completely forgotten about.

"How would we do that?" he said, not worrying about the assignment. He would get up early tomorrow, while his brother still slept. "We love parties."

"But do we love the people we party with?"

"Usually."

"Is that often enough for you?"

Davis rolled his eyes. "Don't get moody. It's cliché for a literature major."

Daniil looked down at his tattoo. "What do you think we'll remember years from now?"

"What?"

Daniil tapped at the Garcia Marquez words on his arm. "What do you think we'll remember?"

"Not tonight, that's for sure."

"Who knows? I wonder if Aureliano thought he'd remember ice."

"That was new and magical to him. What's magical about tonight?"

"Well," Daniil said. "It's definitely new."

Before Davis could say anything, someone knocked on the open door. There stood the vice president. He was tall and Nordic, with cherry red lips that people joked about because they looked like they were smeared with lipstick. Daniil and Davis liked him; he was quiet and smart. He was always smiling, his voice always full of apology.

"Hi guys," he said, hands in his jeans pockets.

"Is he dead?" Daniil said.

"He'll live."

"Tragic."

"What's up?" Davis said.

"Well," the vice president said, rocking back on his heels, straightening his arms. The Goodnight Guys could see the balls of his fists in his pockets. "There are some people who want to leave."

"But we're not at the party anymore," Davis said.

"They're trying to leave and they can't. I said I'd come get you." The VP shrugged. "What do you want me to tell you?"

Daniil crossed his arms. "And we should help because?"

"Come on. You don't want people to be stuck here. You're not that way."

Davis stood, looked at Daniil. "He's right. We're not."

Daniil shook his head but didn't argue. He looked out the window. A girl he recognized who liked to drink Jungle Juice and screech out nonsense to music was standing in the grass by herself, feet poked up against the edge of the sidewalk. She stood in profile, like she was readying for a photo shoot, the halogen from the floodlights on the roof giving her cheekbones and eyes shape and depth. She didn't look discomfited or worried about her immobility; her hands were at her sides, fingers relaxed. He couldn't see her phone, but he imagined it sitting comfortably in the back pocket of her tight jeans. Daniil he let out a small whisper, so low that neither his brother nor the VP could hear it: "Goodbye." He watched something come over her. Her eyes widened, and she nearly stumbled. She looked around, and Daniil felt a warmth in his gut, knowing that she was looking for him or his brother. And then he felt a chill, knowing that it probably didn't matter to her which of them it was that had set her free.

"Okay," he said. "Fine."

They followed the vice president out of their room. The rest of the house's second floor was quiet; a few doors were cracked, their occupants unconcerned about theft or invasion. Someone in the communal bathroom flushed a toilet, the swirling sound leaving Daniil feeling dazed, his drunkenness catching up with him all of a sudden. As if feeling it too, Davis laid a hand on his brother's lower back. They said nothing to the vice president as they followed him downstairs, the sounds of the party trellising up the stairwell, gathering in a warm blanket of music and voices.

The president's complaint wouldn't take. A week after he submitted it, the executive council would dismiss it. He would always avoid the Goodnight Guys at parties, which they would continue attending, except to accept their mumbled goodbyes, which they freely gave. They would play their games of beer pong, take their shots, get sloppy drunk on the weekends and ace their economics exams, polish excellent post-structuralist essays. Eventually they would graduate without another disastrous party. As seniors, the Goodnight Guys would move out of the fraternity house into their own apartment on the outskirts of campus, a townhouse too small for parties. The spell over the fraternity house would be broken. But people would say that PKG parties were never quite as satisfying after that, that the buzz of cheap beer and warm rum was never the same as it had been, that although the hangovers were just as dry and dizzying in the morning, the glowy satisfaction of a raucous night would lose its sparkle when saying goodbye to the Goodnight Guys was no longer required.

But all of that would come later. In the meantime, Davis and Daniil took deep breaths. Their stomachs churned, empty. The VP nodded in gratitude as they re-entered the party, ready to send strangers off into the night.

Glacier

Kim shut the door behind the last guest to leave his retirement party and pressed his forehead against the frame. Stacy laid a hand on the back of his neck like a cold compress.

"At least that's over," Stacy said. "Now we just have to clean up."

Kim groaned and said, "I can't believe I have a grandnephew. We have a grandnephew. When did that happen?"

Stacy pressed his fingers gently against the tender spot between Kim's throat and jaw like he was checking his husband's pulse. Kim stood up straight, smiled, and kissed Stacy on the lips, the heat of his mouth getting sucked into Stacy's. His hands were warm, and Stacy took that heat too when they braided their fingers together. He thought of what the rest of their life would be like, now that work was out of the way for both of them.

But before any of that, before nephews and grandnephews or retirement parties and wrinkle cream, Stacy had once saved the world.

Φ Κ Γ

Stacy: ten years old. His mother: grilling steaks on the stovetop in her cast-iron skillet. Stacy, wanting to be helpful: grabbing the handle like he'd seen his mother do many times before, redistributing the heat because their oven wasn't plumb level, and oils and fats tended to gather on the left side of any pan. His mother, seeing this at the last second: a howl, expecting Stacy to screech with pain. But instead: a tiny hiss as Stacy gripped the handle. No blisters or burns. The only visible mark on Stacy's palm: a faint blue outline that faded as fast as it appeared.

Φ Κ Γ

"The handle," Stacy told Kim, "was cool to the touch."

When Kim frowned and raised an eyebrow, Stacy said, "I'm endothermic. Heat comes in."

They were lazing on Kim's bed. The air conditioning in their fraternity house had putzed out two days before, and the oppression of August in Missouri had left everything thick like potato soup. When Kim, fanning himself with the TV remote, lamented the heat, Stacy wrapped his hand around Kim's ankle. They both looked down at his curled fingers. And when Stacy started to draw the warmth away, Kim said, "How are you doing that?"

Doctors, Stacy explained, had wondered if he wasn't perhaps suffering from CIPA, "Congenital insensitivity to pain and anhidrosis," Stacy said, as if reciting the pledge of allegiance. "But I sweat all the time."

"Yes," Kim said, grinning.

"And I'd have still been hurt." Stacy held up a hand: no scar, no reminder.

"So you're basically one of the X-Men. Iceman or whoever."

Stacy shook his head. "I can't, like, shoot out ice cubes. No quick-frosted beers for you. I just absorb. I'm like a sponge."

"So not a glacier?"

"Not a glacier."

"Glacier sounds more impressive than sponge. I think we should call you Glacier."

Stacy flexed his fingers into fists. "I do like the sound of it."

"So where does the heat go?" Kim said. He poked a finger at Stacy's chest. "Is there a fire raging in there?"

"Good question," Stacy said. Only once had he truly felt the heat moving through him: when he touched the scorching asphalt in Yellowstone at the visitors center, the nexus of his changed life, where he went from teenager to celebrity. Other than that one time, he never knew what happened to the warmth he absorbed; once it crossed into his skin, slurping down past epidermis and steeping into blood and muscle and bone and fascia, he didn't feel it again. Sometimes he would turn on his overhead light or the coils of the stovetop and press his fingers gently to the heat, feeling it slither up into his palm and fingers, trying to track it into his bones, but he always lost it.

"Well," Kim said, laying a hand on Stacy's sternum, "it sure feels warm in there to me."

"Oh," Stacy said, leaning in close, lips nibbling toward Kim's throat, "that's got an entirely different source."

Kim laughed, let Stacy grab hold of him, and welcomed in his warmth, which Stacy was thrilled to give.

Φ Κ Γ

Stacy and Kim married in a quiet ceremony under a banana-yellow canopy—they'd ordered linen white, but there'd been a mix-up with the rental company—in a park just west of the Missouri River, close enough for the muddy smell to purl up their guests' nostrils. After they shared their vows, Stacy went around to the assembled guests—forty or so close friends and family—and laid his fingers on their exposed forearms or the backs of their necks, drawing down their body temperatures so they wouldn't sweat through the chiffon and organza of their dresses or the cotton of their button-down shirts. He did this several times, reinvigorating the assemblage with the help of a bar full of bottled beers on ice and cocktails mixed with booze from a mobile cooler. They danced until the park closed, when everyone staggered to their Ubers and Lyfts. Stacy and Kim were the last to leave, both pickled with sweat; Kim shook off all of Stacy's attempts to cool him down. "I want to feel tonight in my bones," he said. Despite the late hour, they sat on one of the picnic tables and looked up into the night sky.

Kim sighed, saying, "If not for you, where would we be?"

It was true: by then, the world would have been in stark trouble, ashy and dead to rights, had it not been for Stacy.

Φ Κ Γ

Young Stacy became obsessed with heat. Fires and conductivity, lightning storms, pilot lights, gas lines, magmatic chambers. Volcanoes. Sakurahima, Grímsvötn, Mauna Loa, Vesuvius, Colima, and Galeras. He imagined the Yellowstone Caldera wiping out Wyoming and Montana and Nebraska, settling thick clouds of ash over St. Louis, destroying livestock, choking foliage, turning the sky into an endless steppe of gray and gloom. Famine, humans gasping for clean air, world economies tumbling, society collapsing.

Stacy, seventeen: adolescence spent testing his skills. Hands stuck in the oven, his mother yelping in disapproval as he set his fingers on the hot innards that sizzled and steamed as he absorbed their warmth. Hot tubs and pots of boiling water, their roil brought down to the steady surface of a lake by the tips of his fingers. Blowtorches in his high school's metal shop. Scorching engine blocks as cars revved with horsepower and then sat dead to the world. Small fires in his backyard smothered under his palms, Roman candles blanched by his cupped hands.

The news, one day, a horrifying report that swept across television and social media: Yellowstone was rumbling.

Φ Κ Γ

Stacy began cleaning. They could leave the detritus of the party—plates smeary with sugary icing, plastic cups sloshing with final gulps of punch and beer and wine, streamers droopy above the kitchen island, a handful of ridiculous retirement gifts (jigsaw puzzles, a telescope, a Moleskine, golf clubs) stacked on the living room table—but Stacy knew Kim was too much of a cleaner for that; he couldn't leave dishes stacked in the sink before bed, nor let his desk in the study sit untidied. They started in the living room of their modest, open-floor ranch, Kim grabbing a bucket from the garage into which they poured the leftover swill. Stacy stacked cups in one hand and empty plates in the other. Kim held open a trash bag and gathered crumpled napkins and stained plastic cutlery. They moved into the kitchen, where the cake remained half-uneaten on its cardboard slab, the word *Congratulations!* cut off mid-syllable, rosettes of red velvet icing (Kim's favorite) still clinging to the edges. The pan of bratwurst and burgers that Stacy had grilled—who else could cook over an open flame with his bare hands if he wanted to, no worry of singeing his fingers or burning his knuckles?—was decimated, a layer of grease hardened to the tray and holding the last few pieces of meat like quick-drying cement.

They stood next to each other at the sink, soaking and scrubbing because their dishwasher had gone out the day before. Kim would call a repairman the next day, because even though they both had degrees in geology, neither had a clue when it came to stopped-up drains or malfunctioning water pipes. Plus, wasn't retirement supposed to mean you didn't have to work anymore? Kim had spent the better part of three decades teaching sleepy undergraduates, periodically traveling to Colorado Springs to collect samples and study the Dakota formation shale. He'd written his thesis on the Yellowstone caldera after Stacy settled it, and then went to the University of Utah for his PhD, a long sojourn in Salt Lake City where Stacy was able to hide out amongst the Mormons, who, as a whole, didn't register who he was, as if their attention during the apocalyptic crisis had been diverted to other concerns. They spent six years living in a ramshackle apartment with a narrow view of the Wasatch Mountains, surrounded by dry scrub and lots of young men in starched white shirts, Stacy jetting off for conference lectures and lab experiments in Cambridge and Silicon Valley, allowing himself to be poked and prodded and interviewed and documented; a biography of his salvation work came out just a few weeks after Kim defended his dissertation and received his job offer. Over the years, he was offered loftier positions, perhaps because of his connection to Stacy, but he never accepted them. When Stacy would ask, Kim would say, "I like stability."

And Stacy, a tiny grin on his face: "So do I."

Φ Κ Γ

"I could stop it," Stacy told his parents.

They stared at him. Since the timer had started counting down to the end of the world, his mother and father had been curling into one another. At dinner, their chair backs touched like champagne flutes toasting. When they watched the news, full of apocalypse and hopelessness, their bodies were pressed together in bare intimacy, shoulders and hips and knees practically conjoined.

"You can what?" his father said.

"Stop it." Stacy pointed at the television. "The eruption." He held out his hands, palms facing his parents. "You know I can."

His father looked at him and said, "It's okay to be afraid, son."

"I'm not afraid."

His parents had long pretended that he was any other boy. When he absorbed heat, they looked away. If he tried to talk about it, they changed the subject. If his mother was cooking and he wandered toward the stove, she would shoo him out. His father had removed the fire pit a summer ago. When Stacy asked why, he said they rarely used it anyway and its removal made cutting the grass easier.

"Sweetheart," his mother said.

"This isn't a superhero movie," his father said. "You're not a superhero."

"Then what am I?" Stacy asked.

He left in the middle of the night, fishing his mother's car keys from the bottom of her purse. Missouri to Yellowstone: nineteen hours, unless he pushed his pace and didn't stop except for bathroom breaks and gas, which, for all he knew, wouldn't be available because who was still worrying about manning convenience marts and pumps when apocalypse was on the horizon? But he had to do something; he would get there one way or another.

Φ Κ Γ

They kissed for the first time in their fraternity basement, a concrete pit with iron support posts that girls liked to dance around, walls covered in ancient graffitied copies of their fraternity letters. The first party of spring semester, Stacy's sophomore year, was winding down. The lighting was psychedelic, the regular fluorescent bulbs swapped out for black lights that highlighted the neon sprays and sharp whiteness of people's teeth. Stacy, drunk on too much cheap rum, was leaning against the wall near the exterior doors, heavy metal things that didn't ever quite close all the way. Someone had turned off the music.

"There you are," Kim said, slouching up next to him. "Glacier." Stacy's nickname, given by Kim, had stuck, even though it made no sense. Everyone in the fraternity had a nickname, usually a relic of some idiotic behavior; Kim was Puke Stain, because during his freshman year he'd developed a routine of getting so drunk he yakked on himself and then returned to parties with his t-shirts conspicuously sullied.

"Hey."

They had spent their freshman year practically inseparable, and now they lived in adjoining rooms on the fraternity house's second floor, the rent far cheaper than the cost of a dorm room, even if the bathroom was far messier and sometimes downright gross, especially following parties, where all sorts of nasty refuse—half-chugged beer cans, puddles of vomit, the periodic used condom—tended to cluster. Kim was always showing off what

Stacy could do, but instead of feeling like some sideshow, some pet that Kim had trained to do a routine of tricks, he felt spotlit, honeyed by the pride in Kim's voice when he regaled strangers with tales of Stacy's skills.

"You're always here," Kim had said one night, voice gummy with drink, as he defended Stacy's nickname.

"Plenty of things that aren't glaciers are always around," Stacy said. "And the glaciers are melting, anyway."

"But not you."

Kim leaned against the wall, face close to Stacy's. He was wearing a plain white cotton t-shirt, the underarms and neck ringed with sweat. Kim was a good dancer, and girls flocked to him during parties, crowding his body as it wriggled and writhed in perfect timing to the heavy bass and rapid-fire beats spewing from the speakers. He was breathing hard and smelled of something cloying. His lips were moist and glowed in the black lights.

"Good start to the year, huh?" Kim said.

"Decent party, yeah."

Kim's eyes were lidded. "You always say that. Same thing, every time."

"I'm reliable."

"You sure are." Kim's eyelids fluttered. Stacy looked around; they were the last two in the basement. Kim leaned forward and planted his mouth on Stacy's.

Kim's breath was hot and sticky and filled with the acrid taste of rotten fruit. But Stacy kissed him back anyway. His arms hung at his side, half-paralyzed, and it wasn't until Kim pulled back that he could feel anything in his fingers; for once, they'd gone cold.

"Ah," Kim said. "Thank goodness."

Φ Κ Γ

The roads were empty, the projected blast zone evacuated. Stacy stopped for gas, blood pounding in his chest and ears and throat. But the pumps worked. His parents kept a two-gallon plastic gas can in the trunk, and he filled that, too. He wandered around the building and found the doors unlocked. Inside, the place was pristine. Wasn't the end of the world full of broken glass and ravaged foodstuffs? But he was in the middle of nowhere, and anyone who might have wanted supplies could have found them anywhere else but here.

He poured Doritos and Slim Jims and Gatorades into the car. He found a trio of extra gas cans on a low shelf next to motor oil and the condom supply (he grabbed a pack just for the hell of it, his face burning even though he was alone). On his next trip he raided the beer cooler. He was probably on camera somewhere, a security feed catching his rifling and looting. Stacy's cheeks flared again, but then he decided it didn't matter. Once he did what he was aiming to do, no one would call him a criminal. They would thank him. Everyone, everywhere, would.

Φ Κ Γ

When they finished cleaning, Kim and Stacy fell into bed.

They lay in a contented silence, listening to one another breathe, feeling the slight tug of the top sheet as their lungs expanded and contracted. Stacy thought about the days ahead, this shift into a new period of their life together. He could delineate these phases with ease: first their meeting, after Stacy's heroics in Yellowstone had made him an international celebrity, when he decided to quietly attend a small liberal arts college in northern Missouri where people were less likely to recognize him. This had been true: he'd managed to go through orientation and his first few classes incognito, only to have Kim identify him immediately as they sat next to each other in statistics. Then their courtship, Kim besotted with Stacy not for his celebrity but for his intelligence and the way he stretched out his vowels when he was excited or drunk. Kim's postgraduate career in the West and his lengthy and stellar academic life, brought, finally, to a close twenty-five years later.

Kim turned onto his side, hands tucked up under his pillow, his face crossed with shadows and the silvery light of the moon filtering through the blinds. Kim took in a long breath and let out a little cat-like gnarl of gluey sound. "Tell me the story."

This was another of their long-standing rituals: Kim asking Stacy to retell the moment he saved the world. Each time, Stacy tried to clip the story shorter, but Kim always poked him—shoulder, elbow, once his nose—and told him to slow down. Kim said he liked the details; he would close his eyes and nod as Stacy spoke, imagining himself next to Stacy as he knelt and pressed his palms to the hot asphalt. One bustling scientist—young, tow-headed, with moppy curls dampened by the humidity—stopped and blinked at him, and then another. Finally he caught the attention of a ranger who might have thought Stacy was the first of what could have been an endless barrage of crazies, cultists arriving to worship the caldera and the end of the world it would bring.

Stacy told Kim how the heat had been all-consuming, so massive that he at first doubted himself. He felt it, deep and strong in his heart, the heat pressing its way up into his elbows and shoulders, a lactic wave that almost made him collapse. Sweat dripped off his nose, sizzling on the ground. But he could feel the churn buckle just so. He could imagine, at that moment, some nerdy PhD staring at a seismograph or spectrometer, seeing an unexpected fluctuation.

And here was where Kim would take over the telling, teeth flashing, lips parked in a gentle rictus that grew wider with each sentence as he described the scene, one stranger and then another discovering something amiss beneath the earth, not because Stacy was making it worse but because of the exact opposite. Their tilt-meters and GPS monitors were going wonky. The things they could all feel, or had convinced themselves they could feel, as magma built up pressure and the Earth contracted, preparing in days to rupture and sow a chaos that no one had ever seen, were abating.

Stacy flushed as he listened to Kim tell the story. Kim, if not for his life in geology, probably could have been a storyteller him-self. Kim, from whose mouth Stacy's journey to heroics was poet-ry, a hymn, a Gregorian chant, Homeric verse. Words babbled out of him like water skimming low over rocks, a brook of noise and careful, conducting gestures. Stacy could listen to him forever.

"And when it was done, you nearly passed out," Kim said.

"I did."

"And then you were a hero."

"Something like that."

He did not see his parents for weeks. Stacy was pulled into a maelstrom of scientists and reporters and government agents. He was poked and prodded, interrogated in dark, windowless rooms. He did not witness the world get set to right, all of the chaotic dis-order that the impending apocalypse had set off being tamped down. Stacy's mother and father were able to yank him from a bunker in Wisconsin after it became clear he was not a terrorist.

But then the question the world wanted to answer was: what was he?

Φ Κ Γ

Crossing the Nebraska-Wyoming border, his eyes started to itch. More than eight hours to go. The landscape was a dry brown-red, choked farmland and bluffs full of boxelders, subalpine firs, and bigtooth maples. I-80 swept past the periodic truck stop and farm-house, but the route to Cheyenne was otherwise devoid of life. As he passed through the capitol, Stacy saw what the world would come to look like if he failed: barren parking lots, abandoned conference centers, shuttered Safeways and sub shops. He found another gas station as the city faded behind him and managed to fill his tank again, saving the sloshing stores in his trunk for emergency, a thought that made him laugh: what, if not the end of the world, would constitute an emergency?

He skittered through Laramie and the base of the Buttes before climbing through the switchbacks of Bamforth National Wildlife Refuge. He pushed on, peeling north on state highway 287, into the dusty, barren center of Wyoming that was all rocks and bleached earth, carving through the Wind River Reservation and finally into the lushness of the Bridger-Teton National Forest, his first look at thick trees and grass in hours. He marveled that there wasn't more human activity, police or other officials who would try to halt his progress, tell him he must turn back. He'd prepared his defense, brought along with him as many things as he could find in his house that might prove his worthiness: a book of matches, a Zippo lighter, his mother's curling iron. But no one tried to stop him. On he went, chasing after the destiny he knew was his.

Φ Κ Γ

The fraternity house was quietest in the middle of the week, in the middle of the afternoon, when most people were in class or in the library or working their various minimum wage jobs. These were the hours when Kim and Stacy slunk into one another's rooms and sullied their sheets, tangled their bodies together. They weren't ashamed of themselves or hiding anything; half a dozen of their brothers were out, happily making out with the objects of their affection in corners of the basement or dancing up-close with them or sauntering off with them in the night, coming home the next morning to hoots and wolf-whistles and rounds of applause. Date parties were filled with same-sex couplings, some of which were meant to be silly and ironic (the guys who couldn't muster up real dates), others very real (the fraternity vice president, for example, and his boyfriend of a year and a half, who were, without malice or mockery, voted the fraternity's couple of the year when Stacy and Kim were freshmen). But there was something about being able to keep a secret that turned Stacy on. Perhaps it was his youthful celebrity, the way people, after Kim identified him, seemed to always know who he was. They were thankful, but they were also invasive, already aware of his personality, his history, his abilities. When he and Kim dallied together in the silence and secrecy of one of their beds, he relished knowing that this was something no one else could lay claim to.

After, they would lie shoulder-to-shoulder and look up at the ceiling. Kim would raise an arm and Stacy would match him, tendrilling his fingers through Kim's. Then he would draw away the slick warmth that was pulsing through Kim's body. Kim would shiver, the cold suck of vacuumed-out heat like a second wave of pleasure that made him pulse and writhe. Stacy would pull and pull until Kim finally exhaled a heady breath and said, "Okay, okay," and Stacy would let go. Then Kim would press his ear to Stacy's chest and listen to the warmth move through him.

"What do you hear?" Stacy would say.

"A furnace roaring. An ocean swelling. The end of the world."

And Stacy would laugh, and Kim would laugh, and they would kiss, and then they would dress, tingling and alive.

Φ Κ Γ

An hour past Cody, Stacy reached the eastern entrance. He wound through Pahaska Tepee and the crystalline gorge of Yellowstone Lake. Still no guards, no barricades. No indication that the world was bubbling beneath the car tires. The various geyser basins were to the south and west, but Stacy felt he could intuit the heat, it was so vast and tremulous, a beacon whose rhythms beat in the soles of his feet as he pressed the gas, his palms as he clutched the steering wheel, his chest where his seatbelt crossed over his torso.

A visitors center, seemingly abandoned, appeared nearly thirty miles into the park, mashed next to a general store and service station. Finally, life: men in biohazard suits, as if they were handling a radioactive spill. A handful of park rangers, police officers who didn't seem to be policing anything. So many people rushing around like frenzied ants, heads down, eyes lasered on reports or phones or iPads. No one noticed Stacy's car as he pulled into a dusty lot on Fishing Bridge Row. Even when he emerged from the car, in a fug of body odor and sweat, sore muscles and jaw tension, no one paid him any attention. Stacy could sense the caldera beneath him as soon as he stepped out of the car. He didn't quite feel like he was on a bucking ship, but through the soles of his feet, the rumble pulsed, as if a gargantuan stomach was roiling with hunger. No one was watching him. Stacy was tired, his bones feeling scrapy and dense. His eyes were heavy. He had not slept.

He knelt down and put his hands to the hot concrete, which felt like a warm, fresh loaf of bread. But Stacy knew there was more. So much more.

Φ Κ Γ

The morning after the retirement party, Stacy woke first. Kim was a deep sleeper, his breathing wet, ragged, and regular when Stacy was pulled awake by the first rays of sun pushing through the blinds. Instead of slipping from the bed to turn on the coffeemaker or drink a glass of water or release the pinching pressure of his bladder, he turned onto his side and watched Kim's slumber, his eyes rolling behind the lids, the tiny tremors of his pursed-open lips. His face, during waking hours, was always pinched with the slightest bit of tension that was only erased when he was asleep, his cheeks smoothed, jaw relaxed, shoulders rolled to comfort. Somehow, the years had hardly aged Kim. His face was unlined by time, the edges of his mouth and eyes like uncooked batter. Stacy felt his own aging in the joints of his knees and shoulders, as if each bit of warmth he drew into his body calcified in his bones like gout or rheumatism. Stacy thought of what Kim had said years ago, calling Stacy a glacier, and how, really, all parts of life were that way: slow-moving, unstoppable. Most of them, anyway: the end of the world had, in the end, been stoppable.

Kim slept flat on his back, arms tight against his trunk like he was already tucked in his coffin. The bedspread was bifurcated:

smooth and tight on Kim's side, twisted and whorled on Stacy's. His pillow was always moist in the morning, the sheets beneath him damp, and Kim had once hypothesized that it was during sleep that Stacy excised all of the heat he drew in. Stacy had long taken it upon himself to swaddle the sheets in a tangled mass in his arms twice a week and run them through the washer and dryer, using a particular—and expensive—brand of detergent and an army of additive liquids and capsules and beads that left everything smelling new and floral.

When Kim fluttered awake, Stacy said, "Welcome to the rest of your life."

"Morning, Glacier," Kim said with a sigh. Stacy smiled at Kim and laid one of his hands on his husband's cheek. Kim's skin was warm, but Stacy didn't pull the heat away; he relished it, this heat, this body, this person he knew better than any other, even more so than his own. He'd spent a lifetime uncorking Kim's workings, memorizing the muscles, the skin, the moles and freckles, the small bunching of fat at his hips that no amount of cardiovascular exercise could melt away.

"That name still doesn't work."

"It doesn't have to."

"It should bother you more that you're not accurate."

"Not everything has to make sense," Kim said.

Stacy nodded. Life was like that, of course, wandering in ways unpredictable and unbalanced. He roped an arm over Kim's shoulder and they lay close, Stacy pulling in a long breath, Kim setting his fist on Stacy's sternum above his heart. Stacy felt his pulse racing, then slowing, canting along at its cool, regular pace. Normal for now, waiting for whatever would come along to heat it up next.

Florist

Zachary stands at the front of the banquet hall, the PKG fraternity banner behind him. He feels stupid, like a child, holding the terra cotta pot with its rough edges, sixty college guys staring at him between bites of their mediocre ribeye steaks. The pot is heavy, full of soil. Even though he's done this dozens—maybe hundreds? millions?—of times, his hands are shaking. Not, of course, because he thinks it won't work—of course it will—but because of how people will react.

Sometimes they ask how he does it, and he responds with, "How? I don't know." This is true enough. The only secret, if one can even call it a secret, is that he thinks: *I want this flower to grow* or *I wish the grass was greener* or *That oak tree should bloom fresh leaves now,* and he touches the thing in question, or nearabouts as in the case of the pot in his hands, and *voila,* the thing happens.

"So, like, if I handed you a lottery ticket," people inevitably ask, and Zachary shakes his head, explaining that no, it does not work that way. Plenty of people have asked him to try anyway, and he's tried anyway, and it still doesn't work. And they look disappointed, like, *all you can do is grow flowers at will?*

To which he thinks, *Well, what's your special gift, then?* But instead he just shrugs.

The banquet is the final event of rush week, a deviation from the informality of the PKG open house that featured a live band in the basement and a heap of tiny calzones from the local pizzeria, and the casino day where they gave away a new iPhone to one lucky (and much desired, and thus pre-selected) freshman, and the evening at the Chinese buffet where they decimated the supply of crab rangoon and sweet-and-sour chicken. Tonight, instead of their hoodies and Phi Kappa Gamma t-shirts, everyone is done up in Oxfords and shiny ties. Hair is slicked smooth, throats are shaved clean. For the last half an hour, PKGs have talked about various parts of PASSION: Philanthropy, Academics, Sports, Supportiveness, Integrity, Opportunities, and—Zachary's piece—Nontraditional. What better way to prove that you're not like every other fraternity on campus than to trot out the guy who can make a lady slipper grow from nothing to full bloom in the course of about ten seconds?

Zachary does his thing. He gives a brief, saccharine speech about how PKG isn't like the other fraternities on campus. They celebrate National Coming Out Day every year, replacing their fraternity flag on its pole with a rainbow one; they care about grades (true: highest GPA on campus for three years running); they have a buddy system for exams and getting to class, blah blah blah. He knows that no one really cares about any of this; the point is to dazzle, yes, but most of the guys here, on the Thursday night of rush, which ends in the morning with the signing of the bids, have already made up their minds.

Still, who doesn't like a good show?

He has no trouble with the lady slipper. When he wills it to do so, the orchid emerges from the soil, led by the closed white lip of its octopus-like bloom, then the green-black-purple stalk. At first, he's the only one who can see it, for just the briefest moment, while the flower is still bursting through below the edge of the pot. Zachary purposely underfills the soil for this very reason, and in this moment, he feels as though the orchid is speaking to him. He doesn't know what it is saying, but he likes to hear the non-voice in his head.

The guys who don't know what the fuck Zachary is doing let out small oohs and ahhs and periodic gasps when the orchid starts to grow as if in time-lapse video right before their eyes, the flower opening to reveal the petals and anther and column. Up-close, the scent is sweet and earthy thanks to the soil. Zachary stands with the orchid in full bloom, its pinks and greens vibrant and practically glowing. Everyone claps, and Zachary sits.

Soon enough, with speeches complete, people are jawing at their tables, mingling and mixing. Despite the dazzle of what he's done, no one notices when Zachary excuses himself, leaving the pot on his chair, and slips out of the banquet hall, which is crammed at the rear of a gargantuan restaurant that might as well be an airplane hangar. Instead of heading for the restroom, he slips out the front door and stalks around to the side of the building, where he can smell the stench of the dumpster. As if they've timed it, a side door opens and Cody steps out.

"How'd the show go?" Cody says, pulling a cigarette from his apron. Cody has thick red hair he parts on the left and a quarterback's jawline—in fact, he resembles Andy Dalton—but the body of someone who plays basketball and is trained as a dancer. Zachary once admitted his jealousy of Cody's physique. Cody placed a hand on Zachary's chest and said, "Don't be. I missed out on a lot to get it."

"Like what?"

"Sleeping in. Having fun. Oh, and cheeseburgers."

Cody lights the cigarette with a lighter he slides from his back pocket. He isn't in a fraternity, though he did rush at the same time as Zachary two years ago, was even offered a bid by PKG—and three others—but didn't sign any of them. Zachary isn't sure how, but Cody manages to work thirty hours a week while still managing to be a full-time student. The idea of spending that much time hauling cups of ranch dressing and sloshy tankards of beer to the tight-wad locals and the poor college students while trying to also take exams and write essays—Cody is a history major—is stunningly mind-bending for Zachary, whose bio major and desire to maintain a perfect 4.0 GPA keep him up late at night.

"The show was fine," Zachary says.

"What did you grow this time?"

Zachary tells him. Cody nods and puffs on his cigarette. The actual smell turns Zachary off, but somehow the combination of smoke and nicotine and tar, when purled on Cody's warm lips in concert with the slick of his saliva, is an intoxicant.

Last spring, Zachary invited Cody to come with him to formal, a weekend-long affair, alums descending on the fraternity house and partying from approximately two in the afternoon on Friday through two AM Sunday. The house was a wreck, the first floor looking like a disordered recycling center thanks to the many crushed beer cans and half-empty fifths of cheap rum and whiskey and vodka. Cody had begged off, claiming he had to work, even though Zachary told him about it three weeks in advance. When

Cody saw Zachary's obvious disappointment, he said, "It's just not my thing."

"That's okay," Zachary said. But he did feel deflated and let down. All through high school, he'd dragged himself to homecoming and prom solo, part of a chummy group of guys and girls. Although he did manage to slow dance with a few of the girls—and one of the guys, though it was clearly for the novelty—they were sterile steps around the auditorium, bodies rigid, fingers touching shoulders or hips for balance only. He spent most of the syrupy ballads watching his classmates cling to one another, couples whispering romance in each other's ears. Zachary was smart enough to know that most, if not all, of these high school romances would fail. He wasn't concerned about falling into perfect, lifelong love at eighteen. What he wanted was the feeling of a body close to his that wanted to be there, that yearned to know and touch him the way you wouldn't think to touch anyone else. To feel another person's breath nearby, intimately exhaling against your ear. To feel the warmth of knowing you meant something to someone else, that this person would do just about anything for you.

"When do you get done tonight?" Zachary says.

Cody shrugs. He's wearing his typical white button-down, short-sleeved, which shows off the plumpness of his biceps. A vein bulges at his inner elbow. "Hard to say."

"An estimate?"

"Don't you have bids to hand out? Parties to go to?"

"No one would notice if I wasn't there."

Cody laughs, takes a last pull on his cigarette before flicking it into the parking lot, where the end glimmers and then fades against the blacktop. "I find that hard to believe."

Zachary shakes his head. His job is done. Even though he can make the grass grow vibrant and long, set azaleas along the side of the house into bloom whenever desirable, turn the leaves of the sassafras trees in the backyard to green or their vibrant autumn spectrum on command, he is easily forgotten otherwise. More than once he's slipped out of parties without saying a word to anyone—except Daniil and Davis—and the next day, as his fellow PKGs remind one another of the drunken idiocy witnessed the night before, someone will turn to him and say, "You remember, right?" He'll nod, pretending, and no one will catch the lie.

"Well," Cody says, pulling a tiny bottle of hand sanitizer from his apron and smearing it through his fingers. "I only have two tables left. Should be paying soon. Then just some side work. Give me an hour?"

Zachary nods. Cody winks at him and goes back in through the kitchen door. Instead of returning to the banquet, Zachary wanders the parking lot. His car is at the edge, near the long swath of grass separating the lot from the road. He drove alone. Instead of climbing in, Zachary leans on the front bumper, loafered feet pressed into the grass. The restaurant is located on the town's main thoroughfare, a mile or so north of campus, where the residential area gives way to businesses that crowd the state highway: dollar stores, fast food chains, a farm supply company, a chiropractor's office, two dentists, all ending in the large strip mall containing the restaurant and a Walmart and a party supply store. Cars whiz by, and Zachary feels the hot spume of exhaust even from forty feet and a dipping drainage ditch away. The grass is long, in need of a trim, sagging over and starting to go brown. He could easily take care of it, like he does the PKG lawn: one single thought and the stalks would recede, go fresh and vibrant if he wanted them to.

Zachary finally gets into his car. He shucks his tie, which is starting to itch at his throat, and leaves it a snaky heap in the passenger seat. When he glances in the rearview mirror, he sees people starting to stream out of the restaurant. He knows he's supposed to go back to the house for the final vote on whether to give out bids, but he also knows that it's a formality: the fraternity didn't spend twenty bucks per head on guys they weren't sure about. And even if there was anyone to be concerned about, Zachary wouldn't know. He didn't speak to any of the guys rushing tonight. Instead, he was busy at the head table, watching over his pot of soil, readying to make a spectacle of himself.

Φ Κ Γ

When the knock comes on his bedroom door, Zachary leaps from his desk chair and flings the door open, but instead of Cody he finds himself facing the fraternity president. The house is quiet; the bids have been handed out. Zachary's roommate and everyone else in the house are at a keg party in one of the rental houses occupied by a quartet of PKGs who are happy to douse their carpets in spilled Budweiser when alcohol is verboten on official fraternity property, an embargo that doesn't lift until tomorrow at five. Zachary knows the president, who is holding the lady slipper, skips these parties for the purposes of plausible deniability.

"Hey," Zachary says.

"I spritzed this with water because I wasn't sure what else to do with it." The flower dazzles, looking wet.

"Oh."

"I thought you'd want it, maybe."

"Okay," Zachary says, and the president passes it to him. Zachary's room, like most of the double-occupancies in the PKG house, is crowded, even though the beds are bunked—Zachary sleeps on the bottom, because his roommate spends so many nights at his girlfriend's apartment—and the desks are tiny, crammed next to each other. They barely have room for a television, which is small and sits atop a mini-fridge where they keep Busch Light and lunchmeat. The pot feels heavy in Zachary's hands. He looks around the room, and decides the floor will have to do; Zachary sets the pot in a wedge of space beneath the window, between an air vent and the base of the bunked beds. He's not worried about a dearth of sunlight, or too much sunlight, or watering the orchid; if it starts to droop, he can just set his hands on the pot and will it to vibrance again. His fingers are a source of life.

The president is still standing in the doorway.

"Yeah?" Zachary says.

"It happened again."

"Oh."

Someone has been infiltrating PKG property and destroying the landscaping, clipping down hedgerows at the roots and dragging trowels through the grass, leaving long, dirty streaks in the yard. No matter how vigilant and sentinel they stand, the perpetrator always manages to avoid detection. Last week, to start rush, Zachary sprouted an array of dahlias, irises, and birds of paradise along the sides and front of the house, rose bushels of marigolds around the back porch. But in the morning they had all been rooted out, wrenched from the ground and tossed down like garbage.

"I was wondering. Since tomorrow's bid day and all."

Zachary sighs, holding up a hand to stop the president's mewling speech, and says, "Just show me what you want."

They maneuver around in the dark, the parking lot lit by the floodlight affixed to the side of the house. Zachary can see the carnage out front, where the hydrangeas have been hacked away sometime in the last half an hour.

"I already threw away the bulbs. I know you can't just make them disappear once they've been chopped off." The president gestures for Zachary to follow him to the parking lot on the side of the house. In one fell swoop, squatting on the asphalt, Zachary makes all the weeds that have erupted through the cracks in the blacktop vanish, slurped back into the earth from whence they came. He blooms the hydrangeas anew, bulbs popping rosy pink. The grass he shears to a perfect two inches all around the house, fixing the last remaining dig marks. He gives the mulberry bushes extra thickness.

"Oh, hey," the president says. Zachary turns, swiping mulch from his palms. Cody appears on the sidewalk and nods at both of them. The president turns to Zachary and says, "Thanks," then disappears inside.

"Tell me they at least charge you less for rent because you save them on supplies. Do you guys even own a lawnmower anymore?"

"There's one in the shed out back," Zachary says. "How were the last few tables?"

"Tipped twenty percent," Cody says. "Seems quiet around here."

"Party off-campus for the guys who already signed."

"Isn't that against the rules?"

Zachary shrugs.

"So why are you here and not there?" Cody says. He's changed out of his uniform, ditching the hard, formal black and white for a soft blue t-shirt, whatever image was screenprinted on its front faded from years of washing, and a pair of khaki shorts that end two-thirds of the way down his thigh, revealing the thick meat of quad muscles. Cody flexes a calf, toeing a foot in the grass.

"I was waiting for you," Zachary says. He takes a deep breath, smells the sharp, springtime scents of the flowers he's just raised back from the dead. His eyes water.

Cody smiles, but Zachary can see the sourness of it. He gestures for Cody to come inside. The first floor foyer is an open room with scuffed white walls and fraternity composites hung everywhere, often full of gyrating bodies dancing to the heavy rap music they play on the speaker system, clusters of drinkers and gossipers standing in various nooks and crannies, beer pong played on a plywood board set atop a folding table. Right now, the quiet is deafening, the smell of bleach and Pine-Sol from the deep scrubbing the PKGs gave the house at the start of rush still tingeing Zachary's nostrils.

"Looks good in here," Cody says as they cross the room to the stairs. "More model home than party cave."

"We clean up okay."

"I guess you do. No vandals inside the house?"

"Purely exterior."

As soon as Zachary closes his bedroom door behind them, Cody is on him. His body is hulking and warm up-close, and even though he's showered, Zachary can still smell wisps of ranch dressing and fryer grease on his chest. His breath is tinged with buffalo sauce, probably from a sandwich or a pound of wings Cody scarfed down at the end of his shift, taking advantage of the half-price he pays as an employee. The tobacco from his cigarette is still there, too, a hot, lingering smokiness. On their way to Zachary's bed, Cody pauses and nods toward the lady slipper.

"Souvenir?"

"They didn't know what else to do with it."

"There's a whole yard outside."

Zachary shrugs. "It's fine." He tries to kiss Cody again, but Cody presses on Zachary's shoulders, making space between them.

"It isn't fine." Cody's voice is diamond-hard.

"It's just a flower."

One time while lying in bed together, Cody had said, "You could save the planet, you know. Regrow the rainforest, birth endless supplies of trees. Reduce the carbon footprint all by yourself."

Cody's off-campus apartment was a tiny studio with thin brown carpet and a crappy kitchenette that was nothing but a two-burner stove, a microwave, and a refrigerator the width of a coffin. His shower was no larger, and the one time they'd tried to occupy it together had ended with Zachary banging both of his funny bones against the hot water handle.

"That's a lot for one person," Zachary said. "I'm not a hero."

"I didn't say you were. Just that you have resources others don't. They should call you Captain Planet."

"They call me Florist."

"That's lame."

"I know." Zachary lifted his hands and looked at them. Cody trailed his left lifeline with a finger.

"Lots in there," Cody said. "You're not just a florist."

"Doesn't feel like it."

"Well, it should," Cody said, rolling onto his side. "Tell me what it's like."

"What what's like?"

"Doing it. Making things grow and diminish."

"It's draining," Zachary said.

"How so?"

Zachary opened and closed his mouth. How to put it into words? What he did didn't cause him pain. He didn't suffer headaches or upset stomach or nausea. He didn't need to lie down. Bruises didn't bloom along his arms; he didn't bleed. But something was fuzzed out afterward, a part of himself vanished.

"What do you mean, vanished?"

"It's hard to describe. I feel like someone's scooped out some part of my brain. But not, like, literally."

"Hmm," Cody said, and turned onto his side, breathing against Zachary's throat. He let Cody's tongue dig into the soft spot between the bone of his jaw and his ear. Zachary wanted to tell him that what he did with his hands and what happened during sex weren't all that different; when Cody was inside him or vice versa, the feeling was the same, a little giving up of something phantasmal, a wisp that was pulled from the hard, hidden inside of his bowels, and afterward, he wasn't just spent physically but in some other, nameless way, his body a little lighter, emptied. Behind the corona of pleasure and perspiration, the briny stink of ejaculate, something else loomed, buzzing around Zachary's nostrils, something no deep breaths or satisfied sighs could quite refill.

Now, in Zachary's bedroom, Cody shakes his head and starts to say something about the lady slipper but Zachary kisses him again, pulling in his restaurant smells, the coal-bitterness of nicotine. Zachary slides his hands along Cody's back, feeling the braids of muscle, and at his touch he feels Cody relax, let the anger out of his shoulders. His fingers thread up beneath Zachary's t-shirt, their tips a shock of warmth against his stomach. Soon enough their clothes have been shed, and it's not until later, when they're lying in a tangle of sweet-smelly sheets, that Zachary notices Cody's shirt has billowed over the lady slipper, draping it like it is a corpse covered by a shroud.

Φ Κ Γ

Bid day is warm, the sky a piercing aquamarine, like an infinity pool that stretches all the way across the horizon. The PKG flag, a gargantuan blanket of green and gold, flutters on its pole, letters a rich black down the center. Zachary stares at it from his room. The newly-raised flowers are alive and safe; whoever has been after them has not struck again.

When he pulls open his window, the fresh smell fills the room. Cody mumbles and turns onto his side, throwing an arm over his face. Neither of them has class on Fridays this term. Zachary spends some minutes watching Cody, his breathing still regular. Unlike Zachary, he is able to sleep through just about anything—including most of the other PKGs stumbling about last night after they came home from the party—and so Zachary gets to see him wiped clean, unaware, content. He likes to imagine no one else does. Cody's hair is tousled, his body relaxed, muscles at ease. Zachary sets a hand on Cody's bare shoulder and feels the striated muscle beneath his skin, shifting and rising as he breathes. Sometimes, Zachary wishes he could control the flow of blood or air, or the density and movement of bone and ligament, instead of something worthless like flowers and grass. What, he thinks, could he do with that?

He pulls Cody's shirt off the lady slipper, which is still as vibrant as the night before. Zachary slips out of the room and heads to the bathroom, taking a water glass with him. He fills it, drinks it down, ignoring the metal taste, then fills it again. In his room, he pours it into the pot, watching it seep into the soil.

"Is that necessary?"

Zachary turns. Cody is lying on his side, blinking at him. His eyes match the sky.

"Probably not."

"But it makes you feel better doing it."

Zachary nods. The soil has already gobbled up the water, the only evidence of Zachary's work a dark stain on the surface pooled near the stem of the lady slipper. He reaches down and touches the edge of the pot and gives the orchid just a little more verve: an extra shimmer of green, a brightening of the pink of its petals. It costs him, but nothing a quick, deep breath won't take care of.

Φ Κ Γ

The party is a crazed mob of bodies packed in the basement. Everything is covered in perspiration and spilled beer. The house smells of bodies, drunk exhalations and sweaty dancing. Zachary joined in for a while, moving through the basement with a Busch clutched in his hand, not dancing so much as jostling through, finding his way to one of the ratty, disgusting couches perched in a corner where no one was sitting. He drank his beer and watched his fellow PKGs flirt and grind and chug and stumble outside to puke. The basement was a dark mash of neon lights from the pair of disco balls affixed to the ceiling and the black lights that had replaced the usual fluorescents, which made everyone's teeth and t-shirts glow.

90

But now he's standing on the back deck, an escapee from the tinny noise of the basement. His ears are still ringing. He checks his phone: eleven-thirty. Cody should be done with work by now; in fact, Zachary texted him an hour ago, something non-invasive but curious, hopeful, but he's received no response. He pictures Cody sitting at the restaurant bar, perched over a sudsy lager, chatting with one of the bartenders who is stuck there until close even though the place has emptied out. Cody is the type who would keep someone else company like that because it's the right thing to do. Far more important, Zachary thinks, than coming here.

He slips up to his bedroom, grateful again for the absence of his roommate, who is downstairs slobbering over his girlfriend, practically having sex with her on the dance floor. Zachary sees the lady slipper immediately. The stalk still stands tall and rigid; rising up from its base are leaves that resemble floppy arms. But the flower itself has been cut, a clear, sharp shear, the stamen and petals and lip slouchy on his bed, lies across the pillow at an angle.

Next to it, as if he needed the clue, a single cigarette.

Zachary swallows. He sits down on his bed, hunched so he doesn't smack the upper bunk, and then lies down, face close to the still-fragrant orchid. Despite the flower's presence, his pillows smell of Cody, his unwashed hair, the funk of sex.

He pictures Cody, stalking around the side of the PKG house, garden shears hidden on his person, face stoic in the dark.

Zachary touches the lady slipper, pressing its leaves between his fingers. He could easily bring it back to fullness, to life, either in the pot or here, on the bed, stretching a stalk and roots that could curl around his pillow; the president was wrong about what Zachary can and cannot do. Most of them are. He could send roots trellising down the side of his mattress or wrapping around the bunked beds' posts, like a turreted castle overcome by vines. He could send Cody a text, telling him what he knows. Instead he takes a deep breath, pulling in the scent of the orchid, and closes his eyes. For a second he thinks he can feel the earth moving beneath him, but then he decides that it's just his body tumbling with drink, trying to stay centered, to not succumb to the pervasive, endless dizziness. There is, after all, plenty of that, here and everywhere, inside and out, in the air and at the root of things.

Outside, a quartet of partiers is clomping away from the house, hopping from one bid night bash to another down the street. Zachary watches them stumbling, drunk and content. Two guys have their arms slung over one another's shoulders, and they're laughing at something, perhaps the desperate contortions of a stiletto-clad girl leading the pack, trying to wobble and stay upright. The fourth member of their party, a guy he recognizes from a bio lab from a few semesters ago—Zachary has no idea what he is doing at the PKG house; he's a Sigma, his own house a few doors down in the direction they're walking—is clomping along at the back of the pack, hands in his pockets, head craned up toward the stars. Zachary can see the loneliness in his jawline, the desperate search for something in the sky. Zachary cranes his neck, tries to see what this stranger sees, but his view is boxed and blocked by the window frame. He touches the orchid, and then the cigarette, pictures himself gouging them both to pieces, to crumbles, like so much rotting dust. Instead, he bends down to get a better angle to look at the sky, because he knows that the earth will not provide him any answers.

Adam

Of course it would be apples. Ridiculous, Carter thought. When his fraternity brothers found out, they would start calling him Adam or something. Especially after the story he wrote about the Garden of Eden.

The lump appeared on his chest overnight. Carter had gone to bed with an ache along his sternum, which he attributed to heartburn thanks to eating one too many slices of the pizza. His roommate, Andrew, had made them from scratch, adding a hearty dollop of Tabasco to the sauce and pouring crushed red pepper over the cheese as it bubbled under the broiler. When Carter rolled onto his side the next morning, his entire body was throbbing. He felt a sharp pain between his pectoral muscles. When he looked down, his skin was bloated like someone had blown up a water balloon and stuffed it beneath his skin. He threw himself into the bathroom, the fluorescent light burning his eyes before they adjusted. Carter was convinced he had fast-moving cancer or some kind of horrible spider bite that was going to stop his heart. But then, when he pinched his fingers along either side of the tennis-ball-sized mass, his skin split open with a painless crack that eased the hurt strumming through his limbs, and a freckled red Fuji apple popped out. His body zippered itself up like nothing had happened, his skin smooth and clean where the muscles met. Carter, dazed, managed to catch the apple in the basket of his hands before it plopped into the clamshell basin of his bathroom sink.

"Curious," Andrew said. He'd gotten up early to watch coverage of the French Open. Neither had gone home for the summer because they had decent jobs in their college's dusty, tiny town—Andrew at the one nice steakhouse, Carter at the university's recreation center—and they both liked their new apartment. They'd moved in at the end of the school year straight from the dorm where they'd both spent two years—the first as hallmates, the second sharing a room—thanks to generous room and board scholarships. The new place was a spacious two-bedroom with concrete floors and a vaulted ceiling, way on the outskirts. Most of the housing closer to campus was dilapidated and smelled like old macaroni, rotting wood, or sewage, and their fraternity house was even worse.

"That's all you have to say?" Carter asked. He prodded a finger at his chest, where the split was now nothing but a whisper of a pink line drawn down his center.

"We're all weirdos, Carter." Andrew was a few inches taller than Carter but about thirty pounds lighter, his limbs twiggy, his hair shaggy. He had a nice smile and a prominent Adam's apple that bobbed up and down when he chugged cheap bear.

"An apple came out of me." Carter held it up, its skin shining against the light.

"Let's eat it."

"What?"

Andrew plucked the apple from Carter's hand and walked into the kitchen, where he pulled a knife from the butcher block and, before Carter could object, started cutting. Carter expected to feel a jolt, as if some synaptic link still connected his body to the apple, but he felt nothing as Andrew sheared off slices, juice gathering on the cutting board and glistening in the serrated edge of the knife. He picked up a piece for himself and held one out to Carter.

"Well?" Andrew said when Carter had taken it.

"What?"

"Do you want to say anything?"

Carter frowned. "You mean like a toast?"

"I mean like a toast. Yes."

Carter held the slice of apple between his fingers and cleared his throat. "To friendship?"

Right after they moved in together, Andrew had been dumped by his boyfriend. Weirdly—to Carter, at least—Andrew had hardly wallowed in the breakup. There had been no binge-eating or drinking, no long stretches of sorrowful music blasting from his computer speakers, no tears to speak of. Andrew had only asked Carter if they might have people over that night, and Carter, of course, said sure. They'd spent the night poo-pooing Perry, pointing out all of his flaws while drinking Busch Light and berry-infused craft beers. Eventually, Andrew had raised a hand and said, "Okay, okay. He was, in fact, a nice guy."

"Bullshit," someone had said.

Andrew, with the solemnity of a monk, had shut his eyes and nodded. "It's true. The things he wanted were just things I didn't have to give, which says more about me than him."

"Dude," their friend Emilia had said, drinking from her beer bottle. "You're not supposed to defend your ex the day you break up. Why are we here if it's not to talk shit?"

Andrew, standing in the kitchen, rolled his eyes at Carter's toast. "Okay, sure. To friendship."

They ate, Andrew quick to pop his entire slice in his mouth, juice escaping the edge of his lips as he chewed, nodding as if this was the best apple he'd ever eaten. He gestured for Carter to hurry up and do the same, so he did. The skin was crisp, the fibrous fruit juicy and crunchy against his teeth, bright and acidic and, well, the best apple Carter had ever eaten.

When Andrew swallowed, he said, "Dude. That came from you."

Carter nodded.

"Think you can make more?"

"Feels a bit cannibalistic, doesn't it?"

"We won't say where they come from. I can keep a secret."

"Why do you think I would make more?"

But then he did. That night the ache was back, an all-over hurt like he was sick with the flu, and in the morning Carter woke to an uncomfortable pinching in his abdomen. He pulled away the sheets and found his stomach bulging just above his belly button as if a strange, tiny fetus had taken up residence there. As with the first apple, it burst out when Carter stood and went into the bathroom and gave the skin a squeeze, as if he was about to pop a pimple.

"This one tastes even better," Andrew said, not bothering to slice the apple and instead taking a large chunk out with his teeth.

"You didn't even wash it."

"No viscera. It's not like I'm eating your blood."

"Kinda feels like it."

"What, you think you're Jesus now?"

"Better than Adam."

Andrew smiled. Carter had written the Eden story for his Fiction Writing Workshop, a class he'd taken for the hell of it in the spring, after he'd enrolled in an Introduction to Creative Writing class the previous fall for his gen ed block. He was majoring in business, but he found he liked invention as much as studying marketing strategies. In the story he'd written, a trio of fraternity brothers on spring break had wandered into Engelmann Woods in southern Missouri and discovered the Garden of Eden inside the tiny, quarter-mile nature preserve, all kinds of flora and fauna crammed into a single paradisiacal acre, giraffes and lions and macaws and axolotls and birds of paradise all jammed together. As the story unspooled, more Edens were discovered across the globe: in Helsinki, in the peaks of Vinson Massif, at the base of the Taal volcano, on the French Riviera near Antibes. One of the boys—they were all described as such, boys, nineteen, cherubically clean-shaven, arms and chests plump with young muscle—found the Tree of Knowledge and eventually went insane because of how much information flooded his brain when he bit from one of its fruits. The other two bit from the Tree of Life and never aged, falling in love with one another and watching the world's eventual end.

"It wasn't even really about the Garden," Carter said. "Plus, the bible doesn't call any of the fruits apples specifically."

"Not sure that matters," Andrew said, taking another bite.

"Please stop eating that. Or at least wipe your mouth."

Andrew licked his lips.

Carter had taken a draft with him to a chapter meeting, planning to walk over to the library afterward and revise it, but then in the scrum of people making plans for dinner—fraternity meetings were Sundays, five PM, usually followed by a mass trek to the

Student Union building for chicken strips or soggy submarine sandwiches before dispersal to finish eleventh-hour homework—he left the copy of the story in the basement. When he came back for the pages after dinner, the manuscript was gone. Two days later, everyone had read the story, the manuscript left in the first floor TV room, rumpled, the stapled corner crinkled. Carter felt a flip in his stomach: near the end of the story he'd included a fairly detailed, though not particularly graphic, gay sex scene, and he wondered what kind of grief he would get for the precision and attention he'd given the male bodies involved. None, surprisingly, came, though that Friday, at a keg party off-campus, two people complimented the story before soundly destroying him in beer pong.

Andrew, unlike Carter, was majoring in English, though he was mostly interested in Shakespeare and John Donne. He was constantly referencing "The Flea" and talking about metaphysics when he was drunk, scaring off the girls he had no interest in anyway. Carter hadn't been able to decide whether he wanted Andrew to say something about the story or not, because Carter hadn't been sure what he thought or felt. He hadn't spent much time thinking about his own wants; he'd hooked up with girls, with relish and desire and interest, but then, every now and then when he was at the rec center, or at a party, or sitting in class, he would be struck by the masculine beauty of one of his classmates or a stranger with iron-thick shoulders or a diamond-hard jaw. Carter wasn't sure what to do with these quick blooms of warm attraction; he'd never dreamed of men before, never so much as kissed another guy, but something about the mystique, the unknown in what it would be like, drew something out of him, magnetic and hot.

Andrew held out the apple with its pair of missing hunks. Carter shook his head. "You keep that one. Enjoy it."

"There will be more?"

Carter sighed. "Probably."

Andrew smiled and took another bite.

Φ Κ Γ

The next morning, two apples bulged from his left calf, sending sharp discomfort up his leg until he stood and popped them out, a pair of red delicious. Carter felt a small wave of nausea when he saw his skin split and then stick back together, as if sewn by invisible thread or adhesive. He caught glimpses of glistening fat beneath his skin, the ruby of muscle and blood, the sinews yellow and gnarled. When he woke up the day after that with his left hand bloated, he thought about keeping the skin pried open when the apple popped out, but he fumbled it into the bathroom sink. He scrambled to grab it up before it was stained by the flecks of dried toothpaste and slivers of expectorated mouthwash still wet in the basin, so he missed the glance at his inner workings. Every night he knew he'd wake with a new apple, because the ache would return, a chronic, humming discomfort that gyrated through his bones, pulsing as though being pumped along his bloodstream. It didn't prevent him from sleeping, but it did yank him awake early in the morning, when the sky was still dusky with dark. He would find the now-familiar bulge and push it out, bringing along relief from the hurt steeped his ligaments and bones.

Andrew gathered them in an earthenware bowl. He made apple cake, fritter rings, apple jelly, and apple and parsnip soup, the latter tasting like something from *Alice in Wonderland*. Carter was hesitant, at first, to eat anything, but Andrew baked a quartet of apples with cardamom and walnuts and raisins and honey, the apartment blasted with the scents of a crisp, heady fall afternoon that he couldn't resist.

"Good, yeah?"

Carter nodded.

The apples only appeared in the morning, so Carter needn't worry about an eruption while he wiped down the rec center's mirrors or dusted the treadmills. He was able to work out without worrying that, in the middle of a deep goblet squat, an apple might burst through the elastic band of his shorts or from beneath his tank top. Sometimes, he felt the ache come on while he was mid-set, or mid-shift, and he forced himself through one more round of bench presses or another pass with the vacuum cleaner that pulled up the little bits of detritus scattered across the weight room floor before the pain forced him to sit back down and suck in air.

As the apples appeared, Carter gave them to Andrew, who spent the summer polishing and peeling and slicing. Every few days, they sat in their living room and tried a new confection or salad or pie, and each one was tart and sweet and delicious. Carter felt a tilting tingle when he chewed, knowing that he was swallowing back down something that had come from him.

One morning, Andrew juiced a heap of recent pink ladies, the pulpy results poured into a pair of glasses.

"Before you drink," Andrew said, snatching the glasses back before Carter could take one, "I need to tell you something."

"Okay."

"Let's sit."

"Are you breaking up with me? Moving out?"

Andrew shook his head.

"You didn't exactly leave your story behind," Andrew said. "I snatched it."

Carter felt something cold rush through him. "You did?"

"I didn't mean for everyone else to read it. I promise."

"What happened?"

"You hopped down from the bar after the meeting and left it there. I grabbed it and decided to read it." He shrugged. "I know I should have asked."

"But then how did everyone else get it?"

"I let Lyons read it. That was a mistake."

Their chapter's social chair, Dennis Lyons, was also an English major. He was into the beat poets. When he was drunk, he would start screaming out the opening lines of "Howl" without prompting. He was barrel-chested, had played high school football and liked to chug beer, and his interest in Kerouac was either strange or right on target; no one could decide. He was a blond brute who often wore button-down shirts open to his waist, showing off strong muscles and a halo of curly chest hair. He loved to read, often curled on his bed, buried in a novel, oblivious to the festivities mounting as the fraternity house filled with partiers.

But he was also a loudmouth and gossip. Questions surrounded Lyons regarding his own sexuality; he was the kind of flamboyant jock who would slap you on the ass and say something about how good you looked, which could mean that he was comfortable enough with his heterosexuality to not worry about macho normativity, or he was actually fluid and flexible in his attractions and didn't care to hide them. He talked about who had hooked up with whom, had once accidentally outed one of their pledges, and wasn't shy about bringing up bad behaviors he witnessed on weekends, publicly shaming people who didn't pay for keg cups or who tried to sneak out with communal bottles of vodka or rum. Lyons hadn't said anything to Carter directly about the story, but he could imagine him finishing his reading and then stomping around the house, telling people that Carter had written a graphic anal sex scene.

Carter rubbed his eyes, which felt sore. His entire body was stiff, even though he'd slept well. Summer was in its twilight, only a few weeks before campus was filled again with co-eds, freshmen hauling their overstuffed luggage up to their dorm rooms, upperclassmen crowding into their off-campus housing. The fraternity house would be bustling, the grocery stores packed, the quad a flurry of activity. Instead of slaloming through days at the rec center, Carter's schedule would be full of classes. He'd signed up, on a whim, for another writing course, much to Andrew's joy because, it turned out, they would be classmates; Andrew had also decided to make such a foray, and thanks to his status as an upperclassman major, he could skip the intro-level course with instructor approval, which he'd gotten thanks to the professor being his advisor.

"It's okay," Carter said to Andrew. "I guess if I ever want to get stories published, I have to be okay with people reading them."

"That's something you want?" Andrew said, sipping from his glass. A line of froth and pulp clung above his lip. "To publish stories?"

Carter shrugged. "I don't know. Maybe."

Andrew smiled.

"What?"

"Nothing."

"What?"

"It's just very you."

"What is?"

"Not knowing what you want."

Andrew stood and started making breakfast, promising Carter scrambled eggs. He liked cooking way more than Carter did, so Carter didn't levy any complaints or vacuous offers to help. Instead he watched Andrew move around their kitchen, a generous, wide space with nice marble countertops and sleek black appliances and a breakfast nook. Andrew hummed as he worked, pulling out the bacon from its slot in the fridge, whisking a quartet of eggs in a mixing bowl, adding cheese and a dab of milk.

"I really am sorry," Andrew said when the set their plates down.

"For what?"

"Sharing your story. You should be proud of it. I really liked it. So did Lyons."

"He did?"

Andrew nodded, shoveling a heap of eggs in his mouth. "He never told you?"

"Lyons and I don't talk much."

"You should try to get it published. That'd be cool, if you did."

"I wouldn't know where to start."

Andrew shrugged. "That part's easy."

"Oh. Okay," Carter said. But then he spent the day thinking about it as he attended to his shift at the recreation center. In the summer the place was nearly empty, the spikes of the early morning and evening flattened. Carter had little to distract him from his imaginings aside from periodic sightings of people he knew, the Goodnight Guys popping in for a quick run on the treadmill, or Picasso making a go at the bench press, leaving a smear of paint behind that he was quick to wipe away with a towel. He saw himself submitting the Eden story, getting it published. He pictured himself opening a magazine, its pages smelling of fresh ink, the spine crinkling with first use, his name splashed in thick black, his story spilling out like lines of so many ants. He sat at the small attendant's desk, waiting for someone to need a spotter at one of the bench press stations. When the clock ticked over to a fresh hour, he would make a loop around, scrubbing the already-pristine mirrors and wiping down the pads of the various machines even if they hadn't been used since his last sanitation run. In the interim he imagined giving readings, sitting in comfortable wing-backed chairs, a microphone hovering in front of him, bashful, excited listeners leaning forward as he described the Tree of Knowledge, the fauna, the sex. There, he stumbled—not physically; he was deft at carrying his bucket of cleaning solution and a fresh towel without tripping over the ellipticals' cords or the periodic unracked dumbbell—his cheeks flaring at the thought of reciting what he'd written about erections and secretions and bottoming. He wondered at his imagined audience, what they would suspect about him, how much of what he was describing was torn out of his own personal history. Would their eyes scan his body, searching for clues? Would they, if he stood to shake hands or sign books, cleave their sights on his backside, wondering who might have licked or prodded or poked at him there? How could he possibly write with such vivid clarity without that lived experience?

He stared at himself in the floor-length mirror behind the free weights. After his shifts he went through his own workouts, and he didn't slug down as much beer as the rest of his fraternity brothers because he liked his abs. In his own estimation, Carter was pretty good-looking. Always clean-shaven, his body lithe with gym-built musculature that one would call lean; he wasn't overly veiny, and he wasn't gargantuan, clearly pumped full of HGH or anabolic steroids, and his hair was thick—no widow's peak, thank god—and he had strong dimples when he smiled. He had nice calves and teardrop musculature above his knees thanks to his particular dedication to squats.

The ache that accompanied the apples was a soft throbbing throughout his body, as if he'd pulled every muscle just so. Staring in the mirror, he saw no signs of the fruits' departures; every crack had been sewn up, every time, with no scar or consequence. Just that morning his left bicep had split open like a banana peel, spit out a fresh, crisp red, and then zippered shut along the vein that trailed up, a hazy rope of algae green. Carter prodded at his arm, massaging it with three fingers. The dull ache vanished for just a second but then came roaring back as soon as he sat down in his pneumatic, lumbar-supportive chair behind the desk.

When he came home that night—he'd agreed to close up the rec center for the girl who usually did so on Tuesdays—he found Perry sitting on the sofa, he and Andrew on either end, enough space between them to make it hard for Carter to tell whether they'd been intimate before he unlocked the door or if they were fighting. A bottle of Chimay sat on the coffee table alongside two tasting glasses.

"Oh," Carter said. "Hi, Perry."

"Hello, Carter." Perry always said *hello*, never *hi*. His voice was a deep bass, and his letters tended toward hard consonants, avoiding the hissing sibilants thanks to, according to Andrew, a childhood lisp that had taken Perry years to excise. Perry, Carter had to admit, was classically handsome, with thick black hair, a sharp jaw, glittery blue eyes. He was always clean-shaven, and he had the broad shoulders of a swimmer. Carter understood why Andrew was attracted to him.

"Have I interrupted something?" Carter said.

"Andrew got off work early. We got to talking," Perry said.

"Uh-huh."

Andrew wouldn't meet Carter's gaze. He looked toward the television, where a Cardinals game was muted. Then his eyes frittered toward the ceiling, toward his hands resting in his lap. Toward Perry, only for a moment, before staring into the kitchen.

"I hear you two have been baking all summer," Perry said.

"Have you?" Carter raised an eyebrow toward Andrew.

"I have to pee," Andrew said, standing and half-jogging down the hall.

Perry leaned back, right leg crossed over his left, which made him look like an ad executive. Carter had liked Perry well enough; he'd never seen him mistreat Andrew, even if their meeting had been something of a joke: Andrew, working at the steakhouse, had been waiting on Perry and two others, members of another fraternity on campus. He'd overheard Perry's friends razzing him for something, which Andrew sorted out had been Perry's admission that he found their server attractive. That's the word Perry had used, and the kind of language Carter would come to know was the foundation of Perry's lexicon: *attractive.* Not hot, not good-looking, not cute. Attractive. But Andrew had felt the same way, and he had to turn away from them when he heard this while pre-bussing a table full of suit-jacketed men impatient to get off to some meeting. Perry left his phone number scribbled beneath his signature on his credit card receipt, which Andrew had also heard his friends goad him into leaving as a joke.

But Andrew called anyway.

Perry looked up from the couch and stared at Carter. "So," he said. He licked his lips. Another thing: his tongue was constantly darting out from between his lips, poking at the edges of his mouth.

"So."

"You two have grown awful close this summer, it sounds like."

"We're roommates, Perry."

"Uh huh." Perry let out a small hiss of breath and hunched forward to pour himself a helping of Chimay, the liquid bearing a striking resemblance to the juice Carter and Andrew had drank that morning. "Did he tell you why he broke up with me?"

Carter frowned. "He told me you broke up with him."

Perry shook his head and let out a chuff of laughter. He was wearing shiny leather loafers, and light bounced off the polished inner edge as he waggled his foot. He sipped his drink, looked at the glass, and then downed the rest like it was a shot.

"Of course he said that."

"It's not true?"

Perry refilled his glass and Andrew's. The toilet flushed, and Carter could hear the rush of water flowing through the pipes, the apartment's one flaw: any use of any sink or the shower or the toilet created a symphony of noise, as if you were surrounded by a waterfall.

"Why would Andrew lie about that?" Carter said.

"You really don't know, do you?"

"Tell me," Carter hissed. The sound of water had stopped. He could hear Andrew turning the bathroom doorknob.

Perry leaned forward. He smiled, wolfish. Perry had long incisors, almost fangs. He stared at Carter. "He's in love with you, you idiot." Then he sat back, his gaze going over Carter's shoulder. "Welcome back," Perry said. His voice, and grin, had transformed. Perry was nothing if not a performer, an excellent actor.

Carter felt a hard pain between his eyes. When Andrew offered to grab him a glass so he could have a share of the Chimay, Carter shook his head. He said he was tired from his shift at the gym and begged off, eking out a half-hearted goodnight. Instead of going straight to his room, he stopped in the bathroom, where the toilet tank was still filling, a soothing rush of noise. He looked at himself in the mirror. Everything hurt, but nothing was split apart. Nothing, yet, had come to the surface.

Carter tossed and turned all night. He heard phantom noises, moans wafting across the apartment from Andrew's bedroom. Carter pictured him and Perry fucking with vigor and joy; he could practically taste the sweat of their bodies, the hard press of flesh. His limbs pulsed with tight, coiled pain of their own, his fingers stiff and rheumatic. He prodded at himself, looking for the telltale bulge of a nascent apple, but everything was normal. Even when the sun finally peeked through his window blinds and he rose, studying himself in the mirror, he found no evidence that an apple was on its way.

He marched into the living room. The Chimay bottle had been thrown away, the glasses washed out and set back in their cabinet next to the plates and cereal bowls. Carter opened the refrigerator and poured himself a glass of orange juice, the tart sting hard on his gums and tongue. He drank it all down in one fell swoop, letting the pulpy acid purl in his stomach.

When Andrew emerged from his bedroom, Perry came following behind.

Carter coughed. "Morning," he said.

Andrew looked sheepish and, like the evening before, wouldn't meet Carter's eye.

Perry was dressed, hair mussed to half-messy perfection. Andrew was in boxers and a t-shirt; Perry was already wearing his loafers. He put a hand on Andrew's shoulder and said he would call him. He glanced at Carter, the tip of his tongue protruding from between his lips. Then, before Carter could say a word, he was gone, leaving behind the smell of his cologne: a cloying, woodsy spritz.

"Well," Carter said.

"I know," Andrew said. "I'm an idiot."

Carter remembered what Perry had told him.

"No, you're not. You're human."

"Apples?" Andrew said.

Carter shook his head.

"Weird."

"It's all weird," Carter said. He mumbled something about taking a piss, and slid past Andrew. In the bathroom, he checked himself out. He stared at his armpits, at his groin, at his lower back. Everything in its place, which was impossible. His toes, his abdomen, the back of his skull: all fruitless. Carter sighed, let out a long breath. His head hurt, as if he was hungover. What, he wondered, was all of this about? Carter remembered the look on Andrew's face when he'd bitten into the first apple, the way his lips glistened with juice. How Andrew would smile as he pulled apple tartlets and crumbles from the oven, face awash in steam and heat. How he held the apples, every time Carter handed them over, as if they were precious baby chicks. Carter yearned for a piece of fruit, a bloom from the Tree of Knowledge that he could sink his teeth into so he would know what to do and what to say. But all he had was the sour taste of orange juice, the sight of his body that looked untouched, unchanged, and the clanging hurt building in his muscles and bones that would not dissipate no matter how hard he prayed.

Bark

The morning after he broke up with Perry, Andrew woke up with tree branches where his legs should have been. His toes had become roots, dirt-crusted and gnarled, ending in fibrous wisps. His upper body looked normal enough; his arms hadn't budded leaves, and his shoulders weren't hardened to petrified wood. His limbs were the same pale, sinewy things that frustrated him to no end, even after months of lifting weights at the campus gym and scarfing down eggs and protein shakes. Perry had loved Andrew's slim body; he would tell him so every time they had sex, running his hands over Andrew's admittedly admirable trunk, where his abdominal muscles were long, attractive slabs. Andrew had spent years dreaming of bulking up, transforming his tube-sock-tiny biceps into python-like bulges, his tepid chest into an expansive slate of muscle, a dream that seemed impossible to make reality.

His bedroom smelled like wet clay.

When Andrew tried to stand, his vision exploded with yellow and purple bursts. He called out for his roommate, Carter, even though their bedrooms were on opposite sides of the apartment and his door was closed. But a few seconds later, he heard a muffled, "Yeah?"

"I need you to come in here," Andrew said.

Carter was tall and strong; he worked at the campus fitness center, wiping down mirrors and racking dumbbells when douchebros left them scattered about. He also offered personal training sessions and spotted people doing heavy squats and bench presses. Carter worked out after every shift, and his body was a lean, attractive sheath of muscle, his skin a smooth alabaster so that you could see the veins rushing around in an interstate system beneath the surface.

Andrew peeled back the blankets.

"Holy shit," Carter said. "You look like a centaur."

"I am not equine in any way."

"You're going to ruin your sheets."

"Help me up, please."

Carter grinned. He had a wonderful smile, dimples and straight teeth. Where most people were lucky if their nostrils were simply neutral, his nose was narrow, unobtrusive, and worked to his advantage. His strawberry blond hair and blue eyes gave him the charm of a countryside farm boy. Andrew tried not to stare at him too often, especially when he sauntered out of the bathroom in nothing but a towel, knots of muscle gathered around his belly button and hips, shoulders and chest sculpted like they'd been poured from a mold.

Andrew held out his hands and Carter hauled him up. His grip was strong. As Andrew stood, Carter held his hips like he was steering a vehicle or helping one of the geriatric professors perform deadlifts.

"You good?" Carter said.

"No," Andrew said. "Maybe?"

"I'm gonna let go, but only barely. See if you can stand. Do you even have feet down there?"

"Feels like it," Andrew said. That was the thing: his body didn't actually feel any different; even though tree roots had replaced his toes, the feeling of wiggling them felt the same. When he tried tensing his quads, the physical sensation of contracting muscle was still present even though the wizened wood didn't pulse or move in any discernible way.

"Well, this has been a morning, huh? And it's barely nine."

"I'm supposed to work today." Andrew waited tables at their tiny college town's single steakhouse—the one restaurant that served a remotely edible steak, at least—and was good at his job; he knew how to deepen his voice and effect a certain kind of boredom for the cadres of accountants and lawyers and doctors that came in, obnoxious in their requests that their food come quickly because of twelve-thirty meetings despite requesting well-done ribeyes. He knew to be a bit more flamboyant with the crews of aging women who flocked in parties of eight or ten, exaggerating the cock of his hip or the looseness of his wrists to befriend them for the hour it took them to gnaw their way through sirloins and baked sweet potatoes. He was quick, able to dart from one table to another with refills or extra honey butter, and he had an easy time remembering which groups wanted separate checks, who needed A-1 sauce, who had requested another basket of complimentary bread. Andrew was able to easily crowd his arms with sizzling platters, and he'd long mastered the art of balancing three pint glasses in his left hand. He rarely needed to employ the rickety drink trays that were a colossal flood of tipped margaritas and Bud Light bottles waiting to happen.

"Well," Carter said. "Should we practice walking? Newborn colts manage pretty fast, and they have four legs."

"Once again, not a horse."

"Well, whatever you are, better giddyap if you plan on earning any tip money today. Can you even wear shoes?"

He could. When Andrew managed to angle the rooted ends of his legs into his Reeboks, they attached as if the soles were rich soil; he felt like a clawed predator digging into thick, warm flesh.

"Okay," Carter said. He held Andrew at the elbow. "Now baby steps?"

"Baby steps," Andrew said.

"That requires you to actually try to step."

"Okay. Just don't let go, please."

"I'm right here." Carter's voice was cool like an ocean breeze.

Andrew managed to take one shaky step. He had no memory, of course, of learning to walk, but he imagined he was feeling the same unsteadiness, the same rickety tremor in his legs. When he took his second step, the hitchy twist of his hips a little smoother, he felt more comfortable. Andrew nodded at Carter, who let go, and although Andrew wobbled, he managed to stay upright and then take another step. Soon he was across the room, hands pressed to his bedroom window, breathing hard.

"Cardiovascular trouble?" Carter said. He was constantly trying to get Andrew to come running with him. Andrew liked to say he got his cardio from rushing table to table at the steakhouse.

"I'm fine," Andrew said. "It's just new. Like wearing those posture-fixing shoes."

"You know those things are bullshit, right?"

"Right."

Carter frowned. "So if you can walk, what about pants?"

After he tore off his shoes, his slim-fit Levi's came on easily enough, one of four pairs that Andrew rotated through, washing them all on Sundays, when the slime of steak sauces and ranch dressing and white fat had accumulated on the denim. The steak-house uniform required jeans and the company's bright red polos.

"At least you still have hips," Carter said as Andrew dressed. "For the belt-cinching." Then, when Andrew was done: "I can't believe you're going to go to work with tree limbs for legs."

"What else am I going to do?"

"Maybe not try to wait on tables?"

"You went to the fitness center with the flu last year and caused an outbreak."

"There is no proof that was my fault."

Andrew practiced moving in his full work ensemble. While Carter watched, Andrew managed to clomp over to his dresser, where he grabbed his folded lap apron and unspooled it, a trio of still-wrapped drinking straws spilling from the pocket.

"You really better hope no one finds out about this. You'll never hear the end of it. Imagine the nicknaming."

Andrew nodded. Their fraternity brothers liked giving people nicknames. One guy who had driven a hearse in high school was called Mort; Picasso sweated out paint. Glacier could absorb heat, leaving anything cold as death. Carter and Andrew had managed to avoid these nicknames so far, partly because neither had any such fascinating qualities and partly because, following their freshman year, they had slowly shifted their orbit from the bustling stink of their fraternity house to smaller parties at apartments like theirs. The girls who lived above them liked to throw fancy cocktail hours to which everyone wore finery usually reserved for formals or date parties, mixing huge batches of French Seventy-Fives or mint juleps. Ostensibly these were pre-parties, after which everyone would scatter around town to their various mixers and keggers, but more often than not someone would bring along extra cases of beer or bottles of cheap rum and, once the high-end potables had been consumed, the well drinks would start flowing and drinking games commence, most of the attendees barely making it back to their units without passing out or slamming into the building's corridors.

"Your lips will be sealed, yeah?" Andrew said.

"They could be."

"Are you blackmailing me?"

"Not exactly."

Andrew rubbed his face. "Not the dog thing again."

"The dog thing again."

As soon as they'd moved into their apartment, Carter had suggested adopting a dog. The town's single shelter was home to at least half a dozen mutts, all crammed into a small, concrete building with concrete walls and bad lighting, the only sunshine coming from a single high window that had reminded Andrew of a prison cell. The dogs were well-fed and taken care of by a pair of harried women, one of whom was the vet and did all the neutering and spaying. But Andrew had balked: although their apartment lease didn't forbid pets, he hadn't loved the idea of the commitment, the time, the money, the walks, the shit-gathering, the toys that would strew across their clean, acid-washed concrete floors.

"And when we graduate?" Andrew had said.

"What? It's not like we'll divorce."

"But what if we don't end up in the same place?"

Andrew had, at the time, been thinking about his possible future with Perry, who was a year older and would graduate first. Perry already planned to move to St. Louis to do his graduate work in accounting and join a firm in Clayton once he passed the CPA exam. Until the breakup, Perry had hinted that he expected— hoped?—Andrew would follow him there. So the idea of Andrew and Carter taking in an animal that one of them would have to part with had felt like a painful, unkind thing to do to themselves and to a dog.

But now.

Carter was standing behind Andrew, who was looking at himself in the mirrored doors of his closet. In his polo and jeans and shoes, he looked normal enough. He tried doing a half-squat; his body felt the same as always, swiveling bone and tendon and ligament rather than twig and bark. How odd, he thought, that one could undergo such a massive transformation but feel no change. Carter watched him in the mirror, and Andrew watched Carter watching.

When he stood up straight and took a step to the left and then one to the right, both without wobble or worry, Andrew sighed. "I guess we could revisit the dog thing."

"Okay, Dad," Carter said. "Best be off to work, Dad."

"Stop that. I have time for breakfast first."

Carter set a hand on Andrew's shoulder, squeezing his slim trapezius muscle. They first met during rush week, when Andrew found himself sitting next to Carter at Phi Kappa Gamma's formal dinner, everyone dressed up in starched shirts and shimmery ties. PKGs extolled the virtues of their philanthropic work and dedication to brotherhood and watched plants grow. Carter was wearing a baby blue shirt and pink tie, the former matching the cerulean stain of his eyes. His collar was tight around his thick throat, licked clean of even a single stray hair. Andrew was struck by the depth of Carter's voice, something out of old-fashioned radio and television voiceover. He'd discovered, through the stilted get-to-know-you conversation, that they lived on the same floor of their dorm, Carter in the wing next to Andrew. When they joined PKG they started hanging out in each other's rooms, their respective roommates having joined another fraternity notorious for a horrifying pledge season that required pledges to spend three nights a week at their fraternity house and most waking hours, too; Andrew and Carter had ample time to themselves without said roommates.

After eating a bowl of oatmeal and a browning banana, Andrew gathered his keys and wallet and phone in his pants pockets, which were admittedly a bit droopy around his tendrilled legs. He felt Carter's eyes on him as he marched to the door and turned back. "How do I look?"

"Like you have tree trunks for legs. And I don't mean killer quads of steel."

"You're mixing your metaphors."

"Go. Don't be late. Bring home the big bucks."

The shift went as well as it could. If there was a benefit to focusing all his attention on making his legs work correctly as he hauled A&W root beers to a cadre of noisy seventeen-year-olds and spooned out honey butter for baked sweet potatoes, it was that Andrew didn't have time to think about Perry. He didn't have time to think about how he and Perry had celebrated their six-month anniversary just two weeks ago, when Perry told him he loved him for the first time. Andrew had felt a strange crush in his chest, had managed to squeak the phrase back at Perry, his voice a tiny hiss of air. Something had spun around in his chest for several days; he'd not felt himself, his mouth dry as if he was perpetually hungover, his breathing shallow like he'd gone on one of Carter's runs.

Andrew was working his usual section, a trio of booths and two square, low tables. He thought of the leftmost booth as Perry's. Its seat pressed up against one of the server's stations filled with steak sauces and pitchers of water. Perry had sat there the day he left Andrew his number. He had been wearing a ratty sport coat with patched sleeves, as though he was some invalid professor getting ready to give an economics lecture. Sometimes, when strangers sat there, Andrew superimposed his image of Perry onto them as they gnawed at their steaks or slapped pats of butter onto slices of bread. He tried to see the same relaxed fluidity in their joints that was present in Perry's, the way his slouch was both bad posture and affected cool.

Andrew teetered twice while carrying sizzling steaks and steaming vegetable medley, nearly losing a four-top's lunch as he stepped through the swinging door of the kitchen. But he managed to right himself each time without losing anything except, on the second occasion, the scoop of sour cream that one diner had asked for on the side rather than slathered in his loaded baked potato. Andrew returned immediately with a fresh heap and still raked over twenty percent in his tip.

That afternoon, when he arrived back at the apartment, Carter was laid out on the sofa, a hand thrown over his face. He wasn't wearing a shirt, and his ankle was propped on the couch's arm, wrapped in an ice pack.

"What did you do?" Andrew said.

"There was a minor incident while I was jogging."

"I told you my form of cardio was better." Upon closer inspection, Andrew saw that both of Carter's knees were torn up, scraped along the patella and shin. "Looks painful. Do you need a drink?"

Carter shook his head. "Took some Advil." He sat up, careful as he peeled off the ice pack, revealing an ankle that looked a little swollen, but Andrew couldn't really tell. "What I think I need is a dog."

"Okay, okay." Andrew helped him up. Carter wobbled and grimaced but managed to hobble to the shoes he'd left piled next to the front door. He held on to Andrew as he pulled them on, wincing as he slid his swollen foot in. "Maybe a doctor, too?"

"Health center tomorrow," Carter said. "Already have an appointment. Think they'll give me something stronger than Advil?"

"I think they'll give you crutches. Maybe an X-ray."

"Don't say that last part. It's just a sprain."

"You hope."

"Andrew."

As Andrew helped Carter out the door, he felt a brief dizziness at how quickly things had flip-flopped between them now that he was the one holding Carter up. With Perry, there had always been this slight imbalance; Perry didn't work because his parents were wealthy and simply gave him money when he needed or wanted it, and he had always paid for everything, which made Andrew feel weird. Cases of beer, pounds of chicken wings, Gatorades for the mornings after heavy drinking: all funded by Perry.

The animal clinic was a few miles past the grimy dilapidation of houses and barely-surviving local businesses, nestled amongst tracts of land lined by wild grasses and massive oak trees. How strange, Andrew thought, that civilization could basically fall away so fast. They passed abandoned shacks, roofs caved in, holes punched through the rotted walls. Fencing lined these properties, razor wire that had gone limp or posts that were cantilevered over like drunks trying and failing to maintain their posture. Andrew turned off the state highway onto a curving gravel drive that switchbacked around a thick line of trees and emerged into an idyllic-looking hillside where the clinic stood, like a cottage out of the European countryside. In a yard fenced by chain link, four or five dogs patrolled and chased one another. When Andrew and Carter emerged from Andrew's car—one of only three in the tiny gravel lot—the animals began barking.

"I'm surprised you acquiesced so fast," Carter said.

"Acquiesced."

"You never did want a dog."

"I wouldn't say never."

"You wanna talk about it?"

"Nothing to talk about."

"I find that hard to believe."

"You don't want to talk me out of this, do you?"

"Okay, okay."

Andrew helped Carter to the door. His bark-encrusted legs were feeling strong, and he thought, for a moment, that he might have grown; Carter was a few inches taller, but as he leaned against Andrew, he seemed to have shrunk.

The shelter's foyer was all cement, the walls and floors and shelves holding expensive dog and cat food. There was only enough space for two plastic chairs, the kind ubiquitous to grade school classrooms, blue and unyielding. The rest of the room contained a check-in desk that cordoned off a door leading to offices and medical facilities. A second door, on the right, muffled the noise of whining animals. After a few moments of standing there by themselves, Andrew and Carter were joined by a woman in fuchsia scrub pants and a cream-colored blouse that matched the brightness of her skin. She wore wire-rimmed glasses and blinked at them when she appeared behind the desk.

"Hello," she said, voice tight as if they were dressed in black or wearing masks, aiming to rob the place of its pricey kibble and stash of rabies vaccines.

"We'd like to look at some dogs," Carter said.

The woman softened as if they were a blessing from on high. She smiled and pulled a ring of keys from her hip and told them to follow her. As she unlocked the door to the kennels, the animal noise erupted, pups barking with incensed vigor, cages rattling. Languid cats with large eyes and patchy hair blinked through gridded bars.

"We don't typically do same-day adoptions," the woman said. She looked over Carter and Andrew. "But sometimes we make exceptions."

She showed them several dogs, all mutts. One was clearly part golden retriever, bouncy and panting, tongue poking through the bars of his crate. Another was a tiny terrier-like thing with caramel fur and black patches.

"What about the ones outside?" Andrew said.

"They're all either in-process of being adopted or still have to get paperwork straightened out."

"Okay," Andrew said.

Carter was wincing, leaning his weight against a cage occupied by a tortoiseshell cat that stared at him and extended one paw in his direction. He reached up a hand and stuck one finger through the bars. Andrew watched the cat poke its face against Carter's fingertip over and over.

"I'm allergic," Andrew said. Carter turned to him, raising an eyebrow. "Just didn't want you getting any ideas."

"I didn't know that."

Andrew shrugged. "It never came up."

"I thought I knew everything about you."

"Not everything."

"Enough things."

The woman shifted her weight. Andrew pointed at one of the crates, where a dog with a gray snout speckled with white and gray was staring up at him. He had mismatched eyes, one an oceanic blue, the other muddy brown.

"What about him? Or her."

"Oh," the woman said, brightening. "That's Pirate. Our longest resident." She bent down, knees popping audibly, and opened his cage. The woman had to coax the dog out; his legs were spindle-thin but his coat was thick, his torso well-nourished. He had glossy black fur on his back and a vibrant strip of white along his belly, which she rubbed as the dog stood there, ears perked. The woman looked up. "He's very kind, gentle. But you should know that he's got some problems."

"Who doesn't?" Andrew said.

The woman asked if Carter and Andrew wanted to take Pirate on a short walk, and while she gathered a leash and hooked it to the dog's collar, she explained that he had heartworms.

"He wasn't well taken care of in his previous home. He's had some respiratory issues, too."

"How old is he?" Carter said.

"Hard to tell, because his last owners just dumped him off with no paperwork. Six or seven, maybe? But he's well-trained. Knows how to let you know what he needs."

Carter nodded and took the leash when offered. Pirate walked with a slight limp, the result, according to the woman, of an improperly-set bone from some previous injury.

"We're all hobbled," Andrew said as they walked out of the building.

"Except you, it appears," Carter said. He held Pirate's leash. The dog didn't strain to rush ahead, nor did he seem to struggle to keep up with their pace. He kept glancing up at them, tongue lolling out of the side of his mouth, ears raising every time either Carter or Andrew spoke. Carter walked with a heavy limp but insisted he was fine as they walked past the car and onto the uneven shoulder of the state highway.

"I just make it look like there's nothing amiss," Andrew said. He watched Carter's jaw grind, bones popping beneath the skin like tectonic plates shifting. Neither said anything.

They walked for ten minutes, carefully hugging the wide shoulder of the state highway, Carter pulling Pirate's leash close whenever they approached a bend in the road. The dog made no objections. His attention was never diverted by a fascinating smell or the rustle of a squirrel in the underbrush. He only watched them. Andrew's galumphing steps, long and awkward, were slowly coming into a more natural gait; he had practically forgotten that his body had undergone the transformation.

"I think he's the one," Carter said after they had turned back and the shelter was in sight.

"Agreed," Andrew said.

"This has been quite a day," Carter said. He and the dog looked at Andrew at the same time.

"Yes," Andrew said. He looked down at his legs. When they stopped at the shelter's front door, Pirate snuffled around, his snout poking at the threads of Andrew's jeans. He let out a tiny whine and then sat.

"Maybe he wants to fetch your calves."

"Funny."

"You've adapted quickly," Carter said.

"So have you. You're not limping as much."

"Yeah," Carter said. "I guess we're both handling our pain."

Andrew rolled his eyes. "Don't do that." He pulled the shelter door open.

Inside, the woman ran through a litany about adoption. They signed endless paperwork, as if Pirate were a child shipped in from an orphanage in Eastern Europe. Carter handed over his credit card without hesitation when she mentioned a fee. She loaded them up with what she said were Pirate's favorite squeaky toys and even threw in his water bowl and a half-full bag of dog food, all of which piled up in Andrew's arms. The entire time the dog sat calm as could be on the slick cement floor, eyes roving toward whoever was speaking.

"I'm so glad you like him," she said, lowering her voice. "I wondered if anyone would want him."

"What's not to like?" Carter said, reaching down and scratching Pirate between the ears.

They piled into the car, which filled quickly with Pirate's dog smell, a combination of wet leaves and dirt. He panted when Andrew started driving, so Andrew lowered the window, allowing Pirate to stick his head out into the afternoon's cooling air.

"How are you feeling about everything?" Carter said.

"I feel good. We made the right choice."

"You know that's not what I mean."

"My legs feel pretty good, all things considered."

"Andrew."

Andrew let out a long breath. "It's funny," he said, slowing to go around a tractor meandering down the shoulder. "I've almost entirely forgotten about Perry."

"How convenient."

"Sometimes forgetful can be good."

"Maybe."

"I'd say definitely."

Andrew had not told Carter about Perry's declaration of love, the way Perry's eyes had gone moony, his voice full of syrup. How, the next day, he'd casually mentioned their life together, the future. *The future:* a phrase that had sent a hard, hot breeze through Andrew. He picked up speed on the open road. His foot felt like a foot even though he knew it wasn't a foot. How strange the body could be, dissociating from itself.

He pulled up to their apartment complex. Dusk was already starting to break on the horizon, the slightest hint of blood red seeping up between buildings as the sun started to set. The day had passed fast. That morning, when he'd woken up alone and transformed, felt like an age ago. Perry, handsome Perry, whom Andrew had taken a chance on, calling the number scribbled on a credit card receipt, whose voice had dripped with joy when he answered and figured out who was calling. Perry, strong and tall and modelesque, who had doted on Andrew with such tenderness. Perry, who, when Andrew said he didn't think things were working out, sounded broken, his voice cloven by radio static, as he begged Andrew to explain. Perry, who simply shook his head when Andrew said he couldn't, that some things didn't possess language. Perry, who then said, "You're full of shit, Andrew."

Pirate bound out of the car when Carter opened the back door. Andrew watched the dog do a quick jog into the grass and lift his leg to urinate. Andrew laughed. They watched as Pirate finished and bound back to them, collar tags jingling. Without either of them saying a word, the dog lay down on the hot concrete, looking up at them with expectation. Andrew looked back, then looked at Carter, who looked from him to the dog. Pirate let out a short bark.

"Maybe that's what they'll call me," Andrew said.

"Pirate? Dog? What?"

Andrew lifted up the leg of his jeans. Pirate's ears went up and he stared at the wood of Andrew's calf.

"Bark."

"Funny," Carter said. To the dog: "What do you think?"

Pirate panted.

"He approves!" Carter said.

"Good thing."

"Yes." Carter set a hand on Andrew's shoulder. "Help me up the stairs?"

"Of course. Come on, Pirate."

The dog stood. Then, as one, they all started for their home, together.

Picasso

From his second floor room in the PKG fraternity house, Logan can see into the rental next door, where one of the neighbors has set up a treadmill. He runs at night with the Venetian blinds yanked all the way up, giving Logan a clear view. The neighbor is portly, and he runs shirtless, sweat glistening on his skin as it rumbles. It doesn't take long for his buoyant curls to go soggy and damp, sticking to his forehead like a wet mophead. Logan wonders why he doesn't just cross campus to go to the fitness center, where the air is blasted frigid. But then Logan thinks: maybe he doesn't feel welcome there, a sentiment Logan can understand. As he watches, he imagines the sound the treadmill makes as the guy's feet bang away, rattling the furniture, the floor. How the house, if one listens carefully, might sound like it is offering applause.

Φ Κ Γ

Logan's friends call him Picasso, but he is not an artist so much as a work of terrible art. His arms and legs and chest are permanently streaked a tepid gray, a swampy accumulation of color that, when he explains it to strangers, is met with disbelief, so he'll start in on some jumping jacks or high knees or pushups, anything to lather up the lightest bit of froth. That's all it takes. As soon as his body is warmed, the paint begins bubbling up out of his pores. People gasp, want to touch, to know that what they're seeing is real. Logan lets them, smears of fuchsia and magenta drawn away with their touch. "Wow," they will say, and Logan will nod, because when you sweat, bleed, and cry paint, what else can you do?

Φ Κ Γ

Campus empties out during the summer, students funneling back to Kansas City and St. Louis and Iowa City and the many tiny towns in between with their singular stoplights and local ice cream shops. Logan stays behind because his mother doesn't like the idea of him dripping paint on her new carpets or the Zuri sofa she splurged on when he received a full scholarship and his college fund could be spent elsewhere. He watches over the fraternity house and in return isn't charged rent. Logan mows the lawn and touches up the paint where partiers and drunken fights have scuffed it during the school year. He deep cleans the bathrooms, holding his nose when he tackles one of the upper floor toilets that has been used largely as a vomit receptacle, blown chunks clogging its pipes. Sometimes he finds dead bees in the corners of rooms, which have a bewildering ability to sneak in no matter how carefully he shuts the doors, and he's constantly discovering scorch marks on the hardwood floors and burnt fabric on couch arms. Logan has to clean up after himself, too, his efforts leaving droplets of paint on the tile and the sinks' backsplash and dotting the yard like blood spatter. He weatherproofs the back deck and picks up all of the fast food wrappers and empty Bud Light cans that crowd the corners of the parking lot. His body is eternally sticky with paint; it clings to his pores, dribbles down his back and into his underwear. He feels it curl between his toes. After he cleans up, he sits beneath his swirling ceiling fan and turns on his television. But he really watches his neighbor climb aboard his treadmill. Logan nods his head to the rhythm of his footfalls, imagining the tremor going up and down the walls.

Over several weeks, the neighbor transforms. His body starts to tighten up, and he runs faster. Logan watches his legs, which rise higher with each footfall. His arms seem slimmer. One night, the young man climbs on with a new haircut, curls shorn close to his scalp. On anyone else, Logan thinks, it would look like a prison cut, but it gives the boy a fresh face, popping his cheekbones, accentuating the way his throat and jowls are disappearing.

Disappearance: something Logan sometimes wishes for, when he cannot hide what he is feeling, his nervousness staining his clothes, shirt collars absorbing anxious pinks and amethysts, when blue sweat dribbles down, collecting hard against his skin.

Φ Κ Γ

The paint has followed him all his life. When he was a baby, his parents nearly lost their minds wondering why their son's cries were accompanied not by translucent, shiny tears, but eruptions of color that seeped from his eyes and tumbled down his chin. When he was desperately hungry, his wails were joined by tourmaline; when he needed changing, he bloomed like a field of violets. Doctors took samples, swabbed and prodded and poked, and quickly figured out that it wasn't viscera or blood or pus. It wasn't infection or cancer or genetic mutation. It was paint.

As a kid, he would obsessively bathe after any moment of exertion or high emotion, his skin raw and chafed after he went at it with a loofah, trying to rip the color away, the drain in his parents' shower a kaleidoscope of periwinkle and vermillion. Black and white crept between his toes as he sloughed off his feelings and worries. Eventually he gave up, allowing the color to matte against his skin, turning his nipples and bellybutton the now-familiar mushy gray, a congregation of the spectrum he sweats out.

In the evenings he walks to the bars near campus that are so desperate for foot traffic they don't bother checking IDs. Even though the fuggy heat leaves him hued in saffron or tangerine, his t-shirts mottled with tie-dye patterns along his back and armpits by the time he walks into the air conditioning, he likes to walk, feel the concrete slapping beneath his feet. His favorite bar is the Rust Penny, even though the name grates on his grammatically-attuned ears. The place is tiny, only three booths pressed up against a wall, a dozen stools arranged along the oaken bar. The old-timey juke-box that doesn't work—music is pumped in through speakers screwed into the wood-paneled walls—takes up at least a quarter of the standing space. But the drinks are cheap and the pours heavy-handed, especially when Trip is behind the bar.

Trip is in a different fraternity, but the friendly Greek system on their campus doesn't make them natural-born enemies. Their frats host big parties together once a semester and sometimes throw house crawls, stopping at several off-campus party houses throughout the night. Logan and Trip were in the same freshman comp class, and when they first had to pair off to workshop their papers, Trip turned around and, without asking if Logan was interested in working together, shoved their desks together and handed over his draft. When Logan began reading he started sweating because he could find nothing wrong with it. He left a purple streak along the margin thanks to a bead of perspiration that plunked off his nose. When he looked up, Trip was grinning and said, "Does that mean you like my thesis?"

Trip has never asked about the paint. Most people gawk, shyly sliding their eyes away like they know they shouldn't stare. Trip, on the other hand, looked at Logan with unabashed interest, but he also looked without embarrassment: he didn't seem to care to have answers, so Logan never offered them, feeling a hard ache in his jaw, wondering if, should he grit his teeth hard enough, color might bloom between his lips.

Trip tosses a cardboard coaster onto the bar. A trio of girls occupies one of the booths, and a townie—Logan can always tell by the hunch in their backs and the bootcut of their jeans and the flannels they wear even in July—is perched on a stool in the far corner. Logan leans on the bar, elbows smeared just so with yellow paint, his forearms glazed from the walk. Trip tosses Logan a damp but clean towel while he pours him a beer, the head foaming up the side of the pint glass. When he sets it down, Logan says, "Slow night?"

"Pretty typical." Trip is all dark, curly hair and ridiculous blue eyes that glimmer like precious stones. A small scar above his lip—some weird accident when he was a kid involving a poorly-timed leap from a playground swing—twitches when he grins. And he always grins, it seems, at least when he looks at Logan. His arms are muscular, his shoulders wide; Logan's sure he played some sport in high school, but just like they don't talk about Logan's seeping paint, they don't talk about Trip's past, a subject he's quick to sidestep any time it comes up.

Trip disappears into the bar's galley kitchen, which is really just a pair of fryers and a single flat-top grill where, on the weekends, chicken wings and sliders are fried by a local in a grease-stained smock. On the slow weeknights, Trip handles any requests for mozzarella sticks or mini-tacos himself, the bar menu a litany of things that can be blitzed in peanut oil. Logan drinks his beer and looks up at the bar's single television, a gargantuan flat-screen affixed above a mirror, flanked on either side by the pricey alcohols that Trip has told him no one ever orders; the bottle of Four Roses tequila is covered in a sheen of dust.

Trip returns with two platters of onion rings. He slides one to the townie and sets the other in front of Logan, then plucks up a ring, shoving the entire thing in his mouth and chewing fast.

"Hot," he says after he swallows.

"That's what fryers do, I think," Logan says. "They make things hot."

One of the girls approaches the bar and asks for another round. While Trip is pouring, she looks over at Logan. She's tall, willowy, all dark hair and porcelain skin. If she cares or notices the flash of drying paint at Logan's elbows, she doesn't let on. Logan gestures toward the plate.

"Want one?"

She frowns but then leans in and plucks up the biggest onion ring left on the plate. "Thanks," she says. Logan nods and watches her eat. Based on the way she holds the ring between two fingers, as though it's something to be afraid of, he expects her to take tiny, fairy-sized bites, but instead she opens her mouth wide—pristine teeth and a tongue stud shimmering in the bar lights—and takes the entire thing in her mouth. She chews with her lips closed, eyes wide. She nods at Logan and gives him a thumbs up. By the time she's done, Trip is setting a trio of beers down in front of her, and when she swallows she says, "His next one is on me. And can we get a plate of those?"

Trip laughs, and when the girl is back at her booth he says to Logan, "Do you think I should tell her I don't charge you for beer?"

The girls leave at around nine, and so does the townie.

"Too bad," Trip says when they're gone. "You could have hit it off with that girl."

Logan shakes his head and starts yawning, as if the emptiness of the bar has triggered exhaustion.

"None of that," Trip says. "It's early."

"Maybe for you." Logan wants to rush home, see if the neighbor is running; it's about that time. But Trip looks genuinely hurt at the prospect of spending the remaining hours of his shift by himself; some nights, when Logan doesn't have to work the next day, he closes down the bar with Trip, helping stack chairs and sweep the floor. When Trip locks up, they walk back toward their respective houses, always parting ways when Logan needs to turn right to get home and Trip has to keep going straight. Sometimes he pauses and watches Trip marching down the sidewalk alone.

"One more, I guess," he says, and Trip brightens.

When Trip sets the beer down, he says, "You should do a project."

"A project."

"With the paint."

"Why?"

"Something to try."

"I'm not an artist."

"But you could be."

"What would you have me do?"
"It's not what I would do. It's what you would do."
"What if I wouldn't do anything?"
"There has to be something."
Logan shakes his head and drinks.

Φ Κ Γ

His fellow PKGs love the paint. They trot him out during rush, barking out support as he goes through his miniature interval training sessions so that his body takes on the vibrance of a blood orange or the shimmery pink-purple of Roxy Dahlias. Guys gape; girls want to touch. He's a freak, a carnival sideshow feature that, for some reason, convinces freshmen to sign bids when offered, and so the fraternity has built into the budget a supply of clothes for Logan, fresh t-shirts and underwear that he can sully however often he wants or needs, all for the sake of the fraternity's growth. He has no idea why PKG—or the guys rushing PKG—thinks his display is effective and meaningful, but it is, and so he accepts the attention and the attendant duties, even though he has to scrub his skin raw to clear his pores.

Φ Κ Γ

Logan is lucky to work in the enrollment office, where the air conditioning is kept at a high blast. His work—answering phone calls about upcoming freshman orientation, stuffing welcome packets for said orientation—doesn't make him nervous, so he rarely finds himself sweating. He can handle the long, boring days in a way that the other student workers, who are all taking summer classes,

136

seem unable to. They're constantly jittering, legs thwacking against their desk chairs, pencils thrumming against psychology textbooks. Logan likes to stare out the window, which faces the quad, mostly empty except for the occasional summer school student sprawled out on a beach towel or blanket.

Trip appears in the office, standing in front of Logan's desk as if he's materialized out of nowhere.

"What are you doing here?"

"I assume you get a lunch break."

Logan looks at the clock on the computer. "In thirty minutes."

"I can wait."

"You can help." Logan holds out a stack of flyers. "Trifold these, please."

"Okay, but if I get a paper cut, I expect workman's comp."

They fold, the stack of neat pages turning into an accordion of origami.

Trip drags him to a diner where the French fries are smothered in cayenne pepper and salt. The heat makes Logan start sweating, and Trip reaches out, dragging a finger across his forehead, tip stained green. He looks at it with what seems to Logan like yearning and love, and he feels his stomach turn. Logan drinks from his gargantuan glass of water in a red plastic cup that hides the perspiration his palm leaves behind.

"What are you doing?" Logan says when Trip starts dabbing his fingers along a napkin.

"Making something."

"Making what?"

"I'll know that when I'm done."

"You'll get paint in your food."

"That's what forks are for."

"We're eating burgers."

Trip shrugs and keeps smearing his finger against the cloth. When he is finished, he holds the napkin by the edges. "Voila."

"I don't get it."

Trip frowned. "It's you."

Logan rolled his eyes. "That is not what I look like."

"It's impressionism. It's an impression of you."

"I'm not sure that's what impressionism is," Logan says. Trip's version of him is slip-slidey, a smudge of a nose at the center, a pair of fingertip-sized eyes off balance, the right higher than the left. The smile is like a chunk of a rosary, dipped across the face at a near perpendicular to the round, soft chin. "Also, I'm not bald."

"I could only do so much," Trip says, "without taking more."

Take all you want, Logan wants to say but doesn't. He picks up a handful of fries and stuffs them in his mouth, letting the heat seep in and then seep out.

Logan takes the napkin with him, keeping it folded carefully in his pocket until his shift is over. That afternoon he rummages for thumbtacks in the supply closet before he leaves and hangs the napkin above his desk in his room. That night, as the boy runs, so does Logan. He sprints in place, lifting his knees, slapping his thighs with his palms until he feels the paint coming. Then he finds a clean white t-shirt in his dresser and smears his fingers across his back and chest where a bright scarlet has flecked across his pores. He leans over his desk, where he spreads the shirt, making sure he can see the neighbor.

Logan's hand is shaky at first; he lacks Trip's sureness and vision, even though he knows what he wants to paint. It takes a few stabs with his finger, the first few lines shaky and drippy, before he gains some confidence. The treadmill, which he sketches first, looks like it's been half-erased, but he finds he likes this. The boy's body is more lines than curves, and the face is hardly more than a blob, the chin and sliver of nose obvious only to him. But he thinks he gets the legs right, the way the stride is long and confident.

And then another idea. Logan bustles himself through some burpees. He finds another shirt in his hamper and smothers it with paint, another treadmill, this one more assured, sturdy in its shape and size. Then he sketches the boy again, still barely more than a stick figure, but he's bent over, slow, suffering. A tiny strand of sweat cascades from his lowered face toward the base of the treadmill like a string of pearls.

This, Logan thinks, is progress. This is how you capture movement, change. He leaves the shirts on his desk to dry. Logan showers, careful not to drag colorful footprints down the hallway's carpet, which would be a bitch and a half to clean. In the shower, he keeps his eyes open to watch the color swirl down the drain, all that was and all that can be both swirling away.

Φ Κ Γ

Logan sees the neighbor the next morning as he's walking across campus. The sight is jarring, and he doesn't realize who he's looking at until they've nearly passed one another. The boy wears a tank top, hair glowing in the morning gleam. Up-close, he looks older than he does on the treadmill; his features are sharp, cheekbones catching the light and throwing it up across his skin. He wears sunglasses, which make him look modelesque, almost. Logan feels himself go clammy, his skin starting to slime out paint, but the boy passes without incident, not noticing or recognizing Logan at all, who doesn't allow himself to look back.

Φ Κ Γ

Trip's fraternity house is smaller than Logan's but nicer on the inside, everything marble and shag carpet, which, in Logan's mind, would be much harder to keep clean than the hardwood in his house. But, Trip explained when he gave Logan a tour during their sophomore year, they didn't have parties on the main and upper floors. Normally, people were only allowed in the basement and backyard.

"Then what about me?" Logan said.

"Not normal," Trip said. "Honored guest."

Trip gave Logan a tour, ending at his bedroom, where Trip plopped onto a queen-size bed—Trip, somehow, had a single-occupancy, the kind reserved at the PKG house for the president and vice president only—and asked if Logan wanted a beer. When Logan nodded, Trip pointed toward the mini-fridge tucked under his desk, a particle board monstrosity that looked ready to collapse if another textbook was added to the teetering stack sitting next to a closed MacBook. Logan pulled out two cans of Budweiser and passed one to Trip, who slapped the empty side of the bed.

"Sit. You're making me nervous."

"I don't want to ruin your bedspread."

"Thoughtful. You look dry enough."

"May not stay that way."

Trip raised an eyebrow but smiled. "Sorry, man. I prefer my hot dates to be hot." He sipped from his beer. "And women."

"Oh, I—"

"Usually," Trip said. When Logan remained standing, Trip frowned and slapped the space next to him. "Sit down."

They drank three beers each and watched several episodes of *Jeopardy!* on Netflix, Trip yelling out way more answers than Logan, who did manage to get two of the Final Jeopardy questions correct. By the last episode, they were both supine on the bed, heads propped up by pillows, elbows clanging against one another. Logan felt lightheaded, mostly from the booze but also from what Trip had said, the word *usually* floating in his head, a ghostly echo. When he eventually left, Trip walking him out and burping as he opened the house's front door, Logan was feeling a nervy sweat percolate at the back of his neck, but nothing poured out; Trip's bedspread and shams were clean, without a trace of Logan left behind.

Φ Κ Γ

By the end of summer, the neighbor boy looks totally different. The transformation jars Logan. Eight weeks is all it has taken for the shambling neighbor to lean down dramatically. Logan wonders, as he watches him practically sprinting, what other changes he has made: diet, better sleep? Maybe fewer sodas, or possibly Lap-band surgery? Logan glances, at night, at the portraits, now crusted and solid on his shirts, which he's tacked up above his bed. They don't look familiar, even though he remembers with a vivid brightness how he stooped over to dab at the fabric, the way his back ached at the curve. How the paint dried on his fingertips.

He has not shown them to Trip. No one has seen them. He's sure he'll take them down before his fraternity brothers move back in. Too many Picasso jokes. Too easy.

Logan looks out the window, a hollow, hungry ache in his chest. For what, he's not sure, even though he's also positively sure.

The boy is back at it, cranking the treadmill's speed to a sprint. His legs are long and ready. His hair is starting to grow out again, not quite curly yet but definitely going wavy, evidence, at least, that some parts of us are deeply rooted and no amount of strain will excise them. Every night he runs, Logan paints, adding another image to his stack, as if, with enough tries, something meaningful will emerge, telling him what to do if he wants things to truly change.

Honeycomb

The bees didn't sting.

They crawled up Porter's arms, snarled around his throat, clung to his face. His parents had nearly lost their minds when he'd been born, to say nothing of the nurses and doctor in the delivery room, who collectively freaked out when, as Porter emerged from his mother's body via caesarean section, he was followed by dozens of thrumming, buzzing bees who had been hidden away behind Porter, undetected on ultrasounds.

"Shouldn't blood work have caught this?" his father asked, a story Porter would hear many times as he grew up.

"Caught what?" one of the nurses said. "Bees? We don't test for bees."

The swarm couldn't be kept away. When the staff thought they'd ushered them all out of the room, the bees managed to sneak back in, drawn to Porter like he was the most delicately attractive flower. His parents stood sentinel, ready to bash anything that came near their newborn son. His mother, exhausted and aching, tried her best, waving her hands when Porter nursed and a bee came diving in toward his latched mouth, but she hadn't the energy. And they didn't sting, not one of them. "So," she eventually said, looking at Porter's father armed with a rolled-up newspaper, "what is the harm?"

"There are bees," he said, eyes wide behind his thick glasses. He looked like Clark Kent, tall and suave and pomaded. "Everywhere."

When he managed to kill one, splatting it with the sports section and knocking it to the tile floor in a tiny puddle of mealy fuzz and insect goo, newborn Porter started wailing. The crying jag went on for hours, his face gone tomato red, his throat craggy with use, his cheeks and the swaddling cotton soaked with his tears. His parents nearly went insane, and it wasn't until his father threw away the newspaper that Porter started to calm down, hiccupping and murmuring and spitting up frustrated bubbles of saliva, hands whirling around, bees humming as they crawled across his body.

"Well, I love them," Jack said when Porter told that story. They were sitting in Porter's dorm room, a single-occupancy, offered with little fuss by the university when he and his parents explained his situation.

Porter nodded; he already knew how Jack felt about the bees. They'd first crossed paths on the stairwell as Porter, on move-in day, was hauling a laundry basket full of clothing up to his third-floor room and Jack, empty-handed, was trundling down.

"You're covered in bees," Jack had said by way of introduction. But it wasn't a question, or a statement of worry or fear; while most people went wide-eyed and hiked their shoulders, shuffling away from Porter at the first opportunity—sometimes, even, letting out noises of fear and practically running away—Jack's exhortation had been full of joyous excitement, as if celebrating a victory. Everything about him—hair, skin, eyes—was sunlit gold, his black t-shirt tight around lean, muscular arms. Porter had wanted to stop and say something, but Jack kept moving, and a line of students and parents carrying boxes and suitcases was piling up behind him. The image of Jack, the unencumbered smile on his face when he spoke, burned inside Porter as he finished unpacking his things and said goodbye to his parents. He felt a deep sorrow that he might never figure out where or who Jack was. But then, that afternoon, as he headed out for convocation, there Jack was, miraculously emerging from the room directly across the hall.

"Bee guy!" Jack had said.

They sat together at the back of convocation, which was sparsely attended; most of the incoming freshman class must have gotten the memo that even though the orientation packet had said the ceremony was required, no one was taking names. Half of the rickety white wooden chairs were empty, leaving ample space between them and the nearest students. They could whisper to one another without anyone glaring at them while the president and various provosts made their canned speeches of welcome. Jack, without asking, reached out a hand and set it against Porter's bicep, and one of the bees, bumbling along Porter's arm, futzed at Jack's fingers and then climbed right into his palm. Jack was careful as he cupped his hands, the bee continuing to stumble around, antennae wriggling, fuzzy bottom twitching. When it lifted off into a zaggy dance and relocated behind Porter's ear, Jack only smiled.

"They love you," he whispered, and Porter felt full.

It was in Porter's dorm room, after, when he was telling Jack about the bees, that Jack said he loved them. He was going to major in biology and wanted to be an apiologist. He'd read Helen Jukes and Meredith May and had pretty much memorized the entirety of *Dr. Jamoke's Little Book of Hitherto Uncompleted Facts & Curiosities About Bees,* and had even read Maja Lunde's *The*

History of Bees twice, discussing it in his admissions essay, which had landed him a sizable scholarship.

"There's an apiary on the southern end of campus," Jack said. "Though usually only upperclassmen get to work at it." His eyes followed a honeybee that curved up from Porter's throat, took a quick circle around the ceiling fan, and then landed in Porter's lap. "But I guess you have your own hive already."

"No one's ever called them that before."

"Called them what?"

"A hive."

Jack blinked. "What do they call them?"

"Mostly pests. Weird. Bad."

"Oh no," Jack said, laying a hand on Porter's. Jack's chair creaked as he leaned in close. "Never."

Φ Κ Γ

Rushing was Jack's idea. Three weeks into the semester they'd already established a routine of eating lunch together three days a week after Porter's eleven-thirty class, an Introduction to Psychology course. They ate dinner together most nights, Jack making the effort after Porter told him that he'd spent most of his school life eating meals alone: the bees had frightened the other little kids into screaming fits if he sat at their tables, so he'd been shoved into the assistant principal's office with his peanut butter and jelly sandwiches; in high school, the biology teacher understood that the bees would do no harm and offered one of the lab tables in the back of his room for Porter's meals. Jack used the lunch and dinner hours to slowly expand their social circle, telling people about Porter and his bees. These strangers were, despite Jack's exhortations, wary of the honeybees that hummed around Porter and periodically hopped onto one of their shoulders or torsos. While Porter sat silent and hard-jawed, Jack was always quick to tell the besieged subject to just relax, that the bees wouldn't sting unless they felt threatened.

On the Friday afternoon that fraternity rush started, Jack came barging in at three-thirty. Porter was trying to finish his Spanish homework, a series of verb conjugations, and set down his pencil.

"You want us to do what?"

"Rush a fraternity. Or several. Or none. It costs five dollars."

"But why?" The idea had never occurred to Porter. A fraternity was just another opportunity to see strangers balk at the bees, to turn away from him as quickly as they could, attempting to hide their fear or worry or disgust.

"Why not?" Jack said. "It's something to do."

During orientation week, upperclassmen had come through their dorm, passing out flyers for off-campus parties with hand-drawn maps and exclamations about free beer. Jack had gone off to one the day after convocation, and the morning after had knocked on Porter's door and spent an hour lamenting his hangover while explaining the rules of pitchers.

"I don't really do parties," Porter had said and then said again on Friday as Jack tried to practically pull him from the room. "The bees, you know."

Jack nodded but didn't say anything.

"The bees don't like crowds or loud noises. And people tend not to like the bees."

"We will make them love them," Jack said. "Come on."

Porter wanted to say no but he couldn't, not to Jack, with his crooked smile and the tiny gap between his front teeth and the small curls of golden hair on his chest, hair Porter yearned to feel beneath his fingertips. Jack always smelled vaguely of potting soil, as if he was constantly rolling around in the dirt and grass. The loam was rich, and Porter was always taking deep, secret inhalations.

"Okay," Porter said. "Fine, jeez."

"You'll love it," Jack said, pulling Porter from his desk chair. "I know you will."

"We're just checking the fraternities out, yeah? Not joining."

But of course they joined. When Jack singled out PKG, the fraternity whose house was quite literally across the street from their dorm's parking lot, so did Porter. They loved the bees. They weren't bothered by the bees. They hardly blinked at the bees. Even before he'd signed his bid, they started calling him Honeycomb, even though he explained that the bees didn't have a hive of their own and didn't actually produce any honey.

After a chapter meeting, Porter and his pledge brothers crammed together in the chapter room, which was covered in plaques boasting awards the fraternity had earned over the years, mostly for having the highest GPA on campus and for excellent service projects. Photographs of the three founding fathers were affixed to one wall, spotlighted by recessed lighting. The pledges were all sitting around the chapter room's single table, a gargantuan seminar-style oak number. Most everyone was hungover from last night's party, where one of the seniors had brought a bottle of Mad Dog 20/20 that tasted like rancid cough syrup and had demanded the pledges stand in a circle, passing it back and forth, until it was empty. Porter was tired, his eyes heavy, his hamstrings tight. His bees tickled at his ears. Jack sat next to him, one of the bees doddering along his right knuckles. They were discussing their pledge project, a requirement for initiation: some improvement or innovation they could provide the house or their philanthropy—or both—before the end of the semester.

"We could build a beehive in the backyard," one of them said.

"And then we could sell the honey as a fundraiser or something," one of the other freshmen, a member of the college's crappy baseball team, suggested.

Everyone looked at Porter, who blanched. Aside from Jack, he didn't really know his pledge brothers very well, even though they were all expected to be able to recite one another's hometowns and majors and an interesting fact about each other upon request, at any time. Porter mostly had their names down, and everyone except for three of them were from somewhere in St. Louis—one of those being Jack, who came from Sedalia and had the tiniest Ozark twang in his voice, especially when drunk—but he could hardly keep their fun facts straight. Aside from Porter's bees, nothing about their conglomerated group was unusual in any discernible way.

Porter's face felt hot. He shook his head. "I'm not sure they'll leave me," he said, willing his voice not to crack. He thought of his parents and their failed attempts to remove the bees, how his teachers, every year in grade and high school, would scheme some kind of plot—often involving Porter's desk being located conveniently near a window—that might send the bees flying away. None of them ever worked.

His hands were set on the tabletop in hard fists. Porter looked at his pledge brothers, whose eyes wouldn't meet his; instead, as always, they were tracing the bees. He wished that one of them, just one, would look at him, see him.

Jack domed a hand over Porter's. The skin of his palm was warm, as if he'd been holding it up to a fire. Porter looked around the room. Everyone was nodding, or thinking, or checking their cell phones for Twitter notifications or text messages.

"We could always bring in new bees," Jack said. But then he frowned. "Though it's not particularly conservation-friendly."

They dispersed to think about it, scattering across campus to dorm rooms or the student union for dinner or to do laundry or, for those less concerned about their academic performance, to drink away their wispy hangovers while watching Sunday Night Football. Porter and Jack crossed the parking lot together, bees hovering in a tiny constellation about Porter's face.

"It doesn't have to be a beehive," Jack said. "It's probably a bad idea."

"Bad?"

"Everyone talks about saving the bees, but really, honeybees are in the least trouble." His eyes followed a bee tilt-a-whirling through the air above Porter's head. "It's really the native pollinators that are in trouble."

"It wasn't a bad idea." Porter looked down at his chest, where one of the bees was gripping the fabric of his t-shirt. "My parents tried that once, buying an empty hive. The bees acted like it wasn't there."

His parents had tried several schemes to get the bees to leave. On one occasion, his father bought an ultrasonic bee repeller that he tried to surreptitiously hang in the hallway outside Porter's bedroom. It did nothing except stir the bees up into a tizzy, the swarm bopping around Porter's head like leaves in a windstorm. When Porter was told he couldn't play soccer in first grade because two boys on the team were allergic to bees, his parents tried filling the house with cinnamon and peppermint, buying diffusers they placed in every room of the house. The only effect was making everyone's eyes watery and turning them off from candy canes and snickerdoodles for a year.

"I can't imagine not having them," Porter said.

"I get it," Jack said. His voice, as always, was soft. Porter had never heard Jack raise it, even when he was drunk. "My cat died this summer. She was eighteen. My parents got her right before I was born."

"Oh. I'm sorry."

Jack shrugged, but Porter could see the hurt in it, the kind of gesture one might use to avoid crying. "What can you do? She was old. She was sick. At least we knew it was coming." He looked at Porter, at the bees fluttering around him. "Do you notice when they die?"

Porter thought about it. The bees, generally, all looked the same to him. He hadn't given them names. He didn't think of them as pets; they were simply a part of him.

"Do you know how many there are?" Jack said.

"It's tough to track."

"Eighty-three," Jack said. "I counted them once. And then another time. There's always eighty-three of them."

Porter felt flush. They reached their dorm and he could see his reflection in the glass: the bees were hovering in a cloud. Jack smiled and held the door open while Porter walked inside. He felt a tickle at the center of his back. At first he thought it might have been Jack's fingers. But it very easily could have simply been a bee, its little limbs waggling and grabbing.

Φ Κ Γ

The beehive plan stuck, despite Jack's attempts to walk it back. Porter hated the idea of the hive; if he wasn't the single source of bees floating about, what was he? That's all he'd ever been: the boy with the bees. Take that away, he thought, and what was left of him? He also didn't have any other ideas for a project, and he couldn't very well try to tank this one without offering another. And when Jack spoke up, no one else listened, maybe because their pledge class was smart but lazy about it, and once they'd come up with one plan, they didn't want to brainstorm another. Or maybe they liked the idea of a cloud of bees roaming the yard, pissing off the neighbors, particularly the philosophy professor who tended to call the cops on them for noise complaints if so much as half a dozen of them were on their back porch and their voices reached anything above whisper-level decibels.

"I checked the municipal rules," Jack said when the pledge class met again. He looked at Porter with an apology on his face. "There's technically no reason we can't have a hive."

"Isn't the yard a little small?" Porter said.

"As long as it's just one hive, they should be okay," a guy from northern Arkansas with a deep southern accent said. His cheeks were constantly wind-burnt. "I did some research too."

"So you should know it's actually not eco-friendly for us to have a beehive of our own," Jack said.

"We already have the bees," the baseball player said. He was gangly and dark-haired with thick eyelashes. His eyes trailing Porter's bustling hive. He was a pitcher, and so people had taken to calling him ERA.

"I did the math," Arkansas said. "We could buy a premade hive kit with brood boxes and everything for like a hundred fifty bucks. A pack of bees would cost about that much, too. If we want at least one beekeeping suit, that'll run about another hundred or so."

"Couldn't Porter just do it?" someone said. All eyes went to him. "I mean, look. Bees already love him. He won't get stung."

"That's not fair," Jack said. "This is for our whole pledge class. And his bees won't leave him. We don't want them to mix."

"And with the suit," Arkansas said, "it's only, like, thirty bucks a piece. Okay?"

Heads nodded. Porter felt flush. He could see the throb in Jack's jaw, but he nodded too. It had been decided.

Φ Κ Γ

The kit arrived first. On a Friday afternoon, Jack and Porter and Arkansas and ERA stood in the backyard around the brood box, the interior lined in beeswax. It had come fully assembled, so instead of putting its various pieces together, Jack was pointing out its features so they would all know what a queen excluder, telescoping top cover, and entrance reducer were. They would all take turns checking on the bees, a schedule Jack had written up in Excel and printed out, emailing copies to everyone. He'd left Porter's name off, arguing that he couldn't, in fact, participate once the bees had been delivered, because his own bees might revolt and start a war with the opposing colony.

"Is that true?" Porter had asked.

"They can be territorial."

Porter felt one of his bees tuck under the hem of his t-shirt. "They've never seemed territorial."

"Have you walked into another hive before?"

"I guess not," Porter said. "The others won't like me not pulling my weight."

"They'll get over it. You can bottle honey or something."

"You think they'll really produce enough for us to bottle?"

Jack grinned. "Of course not. But our idiot friends don't know that."

The active members loved the idea of the beehive; they waited with angsty anticipation for the bees' arrival. That night, everyone stood on the back deck, staring at the empty apiary. Fully assembled, it stood four feet tall and looked like a pedestal upon which one might set a statue in a museum, the box a washed-out gray-beige. They'd set it in the grass midway between the porch and the back fence at Jack's insistence. He'd also insisted that, before the bees came, they needed to invest in some flowers they could plant along the yard's edges.

"They'll need something to pollinate."

This had elicited a number of sex jokes, followed by agreement and a trip to the only home improvement store in town, filling the trunk of Jack's car with white indigos and black-eyed Susans. He was able to special order some bee balm and purple coneflower that would arrive in a week or two.

"We could also dig out a small pond. More water is better," he said.

"Jesus," Arkansas said. "I didn't think this would be so complicated."

"I thought you did your research," Jack said.

Arkansas shook his head and stomped inside, searching for more booze. Jack grinned at Porter, who smiled and drank.

The house eventually filled with girlfriends and groupies and some of the unaffiliated guys that the PKGs didn't send away because they hoped they might join in the spring. The weather was nice, so the back door was propped open, the sounds of music and revelry pulsing out into the night. Eventually, everyone else was drawn by the siren's call of drinking games and hitting on girls.

"I think they have regrets," Jack said. He was sitting on the porch rail, the hive behind him. His back was hunched over, a beer bottle dangling in his hands between his legs.

"Do you?" Porter said.

Jack shrugged. "I knew what it would really take to have bees."

"You didn't say so before."

"Sometimes people have to see things rather than just hear them." He drank from his beer, the liquid sloshing. Porter watched him hold it in his mouth for a long moment before swallowing. In the night's gloom—the only light came filtering out from the propped door—his lips were liquid, as if he'd spread lipstick on them in a thick layer. Jack set his beer bottle on the rail and hopped down. Blood whooshed in Porter's ears; his mouth felt gummy and dry at the same time. He could hear the bees whirring around him as Jack stepped closer.

"I'm sorry."

"For what?"

"I shouldn't have let them do it."

"It'll be alright."

Jack's eyes slid away from Porter, toward the honeybees hovering around them. Porter watched his pupils dance like insects whirling and swirling through the air.

"We'll need to protect them, I think."

Jack's eyes were wide in the dark. Porter could smell the spritzes of cologne he'd applied at his shirt collar, something flowery and salty. He wondered if Jack knew what kinds of scents bees liked.

"How will we do that?" Porter said. His voice had gone raspy, soft.

"We'll keep them safe," was all Jack said. Then he yawned. "I'm tired. Might call it a night."

"Sure," Porter said. "Me too."

"You don't have to."

"I know."

Jack smiled and picked up his beer, tilting the bottle nearly upside down as he polished it off. Porter's was already empty. He rolled it in his hands.

"Homeward?" Jack said.

"Should we say goodbye?"

Jack shrugged. "Do people ever say goodbye?"

They walked through the darkness, the bees in their usual tizzy.

"What do they do when you go to sleep?" Jack said.

"What do you mean?"

"Like, how do you lie down?"

"Oh."

"I'm just wondering."

"I have to be careful, for sure. I don't want to squash them."

"You take care of them."

"I try. I always feel for them on the bed or my back before I lay down."

"You're thoughtful."

It occurred to Porter that Jack might be drunk. Jack confirmed this by reaching out and tickling two fingers up Porter's spine. Porter said nothing, just kept walking, rounding the side of the dorm, approaching the front door where a bored student sat at the check-in desk, a highlighter in one hand, the other propping up his chin. He barely glanced their way as they swiped their IDs. Jack's hand was still touching Porter's back, the light weight burning like a laser cutting through the fabric of his shirt and burrowing into his skin.

Without a word, Jack followed Porter into his room and tossed himself down in Porter's desk chair. In the hard fluorescent light, Jack's eyes were glossy with drink. How, Porter wondered, had this happened? The bees frittered about, a few landing on Porter's bed, one on his desk, galumphing across his psychology textbook. Jack smiled and followed their flight.

"They dance in the wild, you know. To tell each other where to go, what to do."

"I did know that."

"Bee communication is fascinating. They can say so much without words."

"Probably helps."

Jack looked up at him.

"I mean, words don't get in the way. I feel like words get in the way a lot with people."

"Yeah," Jack said. "I know what you mean."

But did he? Porter wondered. Suddenly he thought of his bees, and the question of how, when, and with what frequency they died and were replaced. How had this never occurred to him? He knew that honeybees only typically lived for a few months. Like the layers of skin his body shed over the course of years, the hive that buzzed around him was in constant flux.

Jack took a deep breath through his nose and let it out. He sounded like a steam pot. Then he stood up.

"I'm glad I know you, Honeycomb," Jack said in a sing-song voice, like he was reciting the lyrics to a country song. He'd never used Porter's nickname before.

"I'm glad I know you, too."

Jack's eyes were moony. Porter's heart leapt at the thought that Jack might kiss him. But then Jack's gaze went to the bees, as it always did. He raised a hand, but instead of planting it on Porter's shoulder, he held it out toward the bees, trying to coax one of them to land. Porter wished that the bees would withhold their affection, leave Jack high and dry so he had to find that love, that tickling touch, elsewhere. But Porter watched one of them, a fat yellow thing, land with pillow softness on Jack's ring finger and then trundle down onto his palm. Jack cupped it there with both hands, his face light and full of satisfaction. They both looked at it in silence. Everything was quiet except for the soft humming of the honeybees. Jack stared down at his hands; Porter stared at Jack. Porter took a deep breath, pulling in the cloying smell of Jack's sweat, which hung on his skin thanks to the heaviness of the Missouri air. For a second, Porter was sure he could smell honey.

"They're so wonderful," Jack said.

Porter, his mouth dry, nodded. The bees hummed, alive, dancing, joyful.

"Yes," he said. "They're great."

ERA

Tim tried not to show his disappointment when his fraternity brothers started calling him ERA. He wasn't surprised that they chose something so boring, something so obvious—he was a pitcher on the baseball team, a team that had mounted a less-than-mediocre 15-22 in its last season—because Tim was, he knew, relatively boring and obvious. Unlike so many of the other PKGs, who sported a carnival's worth of unusual and bizarre traits—breathing fire, or sweating paint, or being unable to get lost, or being followed around by bees—Tim was entirely run-of-the-mill. He even looked it: dark hair, unassuming—though, he told himself, attractive—features, decent musculature, but nothing that would grace the cover of a fitness magazine. And as a baseball player: well, there was a reason he was playing at a Division II school with a sub-five-hundred record and no real hopes of any championships, conference or national. His teammates spent their free time downing cheap beer at the bar notorious for not carding student athletes, and it showed in their performance on the field, much to the chagrin of the coaching staff that had to spend half of their time lambasting the infielders for their hungover sluggishness. One time, the catcher Tim was warming up with had actually thrown up into his face mask, and the head coach had sent them all home early, fingers pinched at the bridge of his nose.

Most of the baseball players joined the Sigmas, their house separated from the PKGs by a ramshackle rental, one of the last vestiges of residential housing on the unofficial fraternity row that backed up against the school's four dormitories. Girls flocked to their parties because, at midnight, the Sigma pledges were required to dance along to "Girls Just Wanna Have Fun" and do a striptease, actives dousing them with skunky beer and the periodic bottle of ketchup if they were too slow in pulling off their jeans. Sigmas were known for their abs and nice shoulders, and the cheap beer that smeared over their muscles made them glisten like professionals. They were usually blacked out by then, their sexy dances more like apish parading, but the sight was popular and usually resulted in videos and photos that made their way onto social media. Tim hadn't been impressed by their house, which was a run-down ranch with bare floors and an omnipresent smell of days-old vomit. Their pool table was covered in suspicious stains, and he had avoided, during the one event he attended during rush, leaning against any of the furniture.

The PKGs were a wonder by comparison. Instead of flaunting how frequently they played beer pong, they trotted out their most interesting members, like the one they called Meat Lover, who could speak to food and receive instruction on how to cook it to perfection, or the senior who absorbed warmth, able to grill without tongs or spatula, raking his fingers over the coals, literally, to turn bratwursts or flip burgers. During the final rush event, a formal shirt-and-tie dinner at the one nice banquet hall in town, a sophomore nicknamed Florist stood at the front of the room while everyone else smeared their rolls with leftover gravy and gnawed on mass-produced slabs of turkey. Florist held a terra cotta planter full of potting soil in his hands. Tim and the rest of the room were silent as he looked over the assembled men in their shimmering blue ties and wrinkled oxford shirts. After a moment, a bright pink lady slipper rose out of the dirt and unfurled as if caught in time-lapse video. Tim felt a flare of intrigue and a sudden surge of knowing that he was in the right place, even if all he could do was throw mediocre fastballs and an average splitter.

The nicknaming ceremony took place a month into pledge season in the damp PKG basement. The floor, acid-washed cement, was sticky. Tim and his dozen pledge brothers stood in a half-circle in the dark, the only light coming from an old-fashioned oil lantern reminiscent of a genie's lamp that was sitting on a folding table occupied by the fraternity president and pledge warden. Behind them loomed their brotherhood mentors, actives who showed them the ropes and bought them beer. One by one, the pledge warden called them to step forward and receive their nicknames. Tim watched as his pledge brothers were christened: the one with scales up and down his biceps was named Boa Constrictor; Michael, who could breathe underwater, was called Mermaid; the guy next to Tim, whose hair shimmered and shifted color depending on the weather, became Rainbow. Finally, then, Tim: ERA. He nodded, accepted the boring name, and stepped back. He listened to the others, watched Grayscale—whose entire body looked as if it had been pulled out of an old episode of *I Love Lucy*—receive his name. Though the light was catacomb gloomy, Tim could see the wry excitement on his pledge brothers' faces at the embracing of their unusual features. When drunk, they tended to show off their skills (Grayscale could turn girls' arms gunmetal, and they shrieked and leaned into him; Boa Constrictor would flex, the hard glimmer of his arms as shiny as precious gems under their house's hot lights), or they would joyously tell stories from their childhoods, laughing at how their freakishness had made them outcasts, drumming up sympathy from inebriated co-eds who would paw at them all evening and wander home with them. Tim, when approached, would say something about being on the baseball team, and even the least sports-enthusiastic undergraduates knew that this was nothing shimmery or shiny, no braggart's boast. He would shrug, sometimes limply offer to teach a stranger how to throw a decent cutter, and then get himself nice and toasty on cheap beer before stumbling back to his dorm room by himself.

The nicknaming ceremony was always followed by a kegger even though campus rules technically forbade "common source" consumption in official Greek housing. A large part of being in a fraternity, Tim had discovered quickly, was figuring out how to follow the technicalities while, in many ways, not following them; in the case of the keg, it was wheeled around the back side of the house, through the grass, and into a small copse of trees separating the PKG yard from the neighbors'. The little stand of oaks was technically past the property line. The guys, who lived in the tiny white shack with a Florida room full of old bicycles and bags of beer cans, were cool with the arrangement so long as they were allowed free access to a plastic cup and all the Natural Light they might want to siphon from the PKGs during their festivities. A small price, the fraternity agreed, for silence and compliance.

Tim hung around long enough to accept slaps on the back, orders to slam beer and acclimate to his boring nickname. Thankfully, no one made much inquiry into Tim's. No one wondered what his earned run average actually was, which was a blessing because he didn't have one: he hadn't actually pitched in a game yet. This was the hardest, most painful knot that blossomed in his belly at the thought of his nickname: his fellow PKGs didn't realize that he was a backup pitcher, waiting in the wings for an opportunity to show what he could do, which, Tim admitted to himself, probably wasn't much.

He left the party early and decided to walk to the downtown square, which was only ten minutes away, even for a drunk, slow walker like Tim; town was tiny, the streets all pedestrian-friendly and largely empty at eleven. The bar, north of the county courthouse and buttressed by a dress shop and a consignment store, was a bit of odd construction, the entrance depressed inward relative to the rest of the storefronts, the glass walls angled inward like a funnel toward the tinted door. Pitchers, the place was called, a reference not to Tim's position on the baseball team but to the liquid container, which the bar served at incredibly cheap prices—only five bucks a pop—while charging fifty cents per frosted glass (room-temperature plastic cups were free). The interior was a weird amalgamation of a fifties diner and an elegant tap room, one half lined with red leatherette booths that sparkled under the hot, bright recessed lighting, the other half taken up by a dark oak bar top with heavy stools. The lights above the bar itself were lowered to a whisper of illumination, so shadowy that one had to squint to read the beer taps, which were all cheap brews except for one, which rotated seasonally through various craft IPAs and hefeweizens that the few professors who occasioned into Pitchers ordered at four dollars a pint.

Tim was hardly surprised to find a trio of Sigmas, juniors from the baseball team, slumped in the booth closest to the door, two full pitchers on their table. One of them sighted Tim the moment he walked in, and all three gave out limp hoots of greeting. Campus was small, and Greek life was more of a big family living in different quarters than a cesspool of feuds and hatreds, so even though Tim had bucked the baseball team's trend, it had hardly made him an outcast. These three, in particular, had remained as friendly and brotherly and affectionate as if he'd joined up with them.

He slid into the booth next to Spencer, another pitcher, who was all elbows and grungy facial hair. None of these guys had nicknames he had to memorize or compare to his own. They were hunched over their beers, glassy-eyed, and he wondered how many pitchers had preceded the pair purling condensation down their sides. Spencer slid his empty glass toward Tim, who took it and refilled it, but when he went to slide it back, Spencer said, "No, man, drink."

Tim did. He'd had enough beer for the night at the PKG house, but he knocked back half the pint before he stopped, then refilled it and handed it to Spencer. The other Sigmas smiled and cheered. On the other side of the booth, Dave and Cal, fraternal twin brothers who played shortstop and right field respectively, nodded. Music was being pumped in through speakers, but Pitchers kept the volume down so people didn't have to shout their throats raw to talk; Tim could barely make out the thread of Journey's "Don't Stop Believin'." Dave, the taller twin, seemed to be listening to the music, his index finger knocking the beat on the table. Cal squinted in Tim's direction. He was the good-looking one, with broad shoulders and striking blue eyes and the kind of nose that fell somewhere pleasantly between aquiline and button. He had high cheekbones and was the one guy on the team who looked like he belonged on a real baseball team, his thighs impressive in his pro-flares. They'd had one odd encounter in the locker room, on a swelter of a day on which Tim took an extra long time in the shower, willing his body to cool down; he could feel sweat still seeping out as he hung his head beneath the flow of water. When he finally dragged himself out, he and Cal were the only ones left in the locker room. Cal sat naked on the bench in front of his locker, and when Tim stepped out of the shower, wet towel laced around his hips, Cal looked up at him. He was mixing a protein shake in a clear thermos, a mixing ball rattling inside.

"Hey," Cal said. Their lockers were near one another, and Tim, avoiding looking directly at Cal's naked body, nodded, stepping over to his combination lock. He was maybe five feet away from Cal, enough space that when Cal's fingers brushed his thigh, it couldn't have been an accident. Tim felt a white heat surge through him, and he held his breath. The touch wasn't followed by a second, and when Tim finally looked, Cal was pulling on his underwear with one hand, slurping up chalky protein shake with the other. He winked at Tim. Cal wore a silver necklace with a circular medallion whose meaning eluded Tim, and that winked in the light, too. Then Cal turned around and rooted in his bag for the rest of his clothes, the outline of his powerful glutes obvious through the elastic of his boxer briefs.

Tim drank some more and Cal was quick to fill the glass. He could feel the warmth of Cal's body, the simple size of it, emanating from beneath the booth. For a quick second their feet touched, and Tim was quick to drag his tennis shoe back.

He turned to Dave and Spencer. "Got my nickname tonight."

"Right," Dave said. "You guys do that."

"What are they calling you?" Cal said.

Tim told them. Spencer snorted. Dave rolled his eyes.

The table fell into a lull. Spencer said something about ordering more beer, but Dave let out a soft, wet belch that reeked of dairy and sliced a finger along his throat. "I think I'm cashed, man."

"Pussy," Spencer said, but made no other objection. They finished off the last of the beer in silence, Dave bobbing his head to the music, "Separate Ways" followed by "Faithfully" and "Lovin', Touchin', Squeezin'," during which Tim felt Cal's knee pop against his. Tim felt a hot pinch in his bladder. He stood, chugging the last dregs of his beer, and said he had to take a piss. The bathroom at Pitcher's was gross, the terra cotta floor always slippery with spilled drinks and misdirected urine, and the urinals smelled heavily of antiseptic, the blue cakes deposited at the bottoms reeking of chemicals. The men's room contained two stalls, one of which was always out of order, clogged up with toilet paper and beer shits. The soap dispensers were empty half the time, which led Tim to question the sanitation of touching just about anything in the place.

When he returned to the booth, Cal was the only one left.

"Where'd everybody go?" Tim said.

"Home. Sit."

Cal was leaning against the wall, feet propped on the leatherette booth. Tim slid in across from him. Someone had removed their pint glasses and the empty pitchers and in front of him, instead, was a rum and coke.

"A nightcap."

"Okay," Tim said, even though he was exhausted, his stomach bloated. He had a class at nine in the morning, and then an afternoon practice with strength conditioning. But Cal was drinking, his eyes twinkly in the light, and Tim didn't want to go back to his dorm room. He wondered, briefly, if any of his pledge brothers had noticed his quiet absence, or if they were too busy regaling drunk girls with their nicknames, showing off their mystiques, their magics, their thrills.

Tim drank, surprised by how much rum was in the glass. He let out a sputter.

"So tell me something," Cal said, sitting up and lowering his elbows to the table, canting forward so his fingers were near Tim's. Tim remembered the hot touch of Cal's fingertips along the tender side of his thigh, a place he'd barely ever been touched before. It had practically scalded, sending a jolt through his center, hot and cutting and then evaporating as fast as it had appeared.

"Tell you what?"

"Why PKG?"

"What do you mean?"

"Oh, come on." Cal stretched his arms above his head like a cat and let out a yawn. Then he steepled his fingers together and dropped them back onto the table, rattling their drinks. Ice danced in Tim's glass. "Everyone knows that athletes join Sigma. Don't get me wrong. The PKGs are nice guys. But they're for the weird ones. The guys with something unusual about them."

"The freaks."

"I didn't say that." Cal took a drink. "I think they're cool and different. Really, I do. But they're not baseball players."

"Am I a baseball player if I never play?"

Cal rolled his eyes. "We went over this, didn't we?"

"It's easy for you to say. You're a star."

Cal let out a roar of laughter. "Look at where we are, man. None of us are stars."

"Then maybe we're all freaks."

They finished their drinks. On their way out, Cal waved to the bartender, who flourished a dirtied towel in their direction. The night had cooled some, the Missouri humidity breaking and leaving behind a pleasant breeze, a starlit sky, and quiet streets. Without a word they started walking back toward campus, the only sound the clomp of their feet. Cal said nothing when they passed Tim's dorm and Tim didn't peel off toward home. When they approached the PKG house, Tim saw that the first floor windows were still brightly lit, shadowy bodies moving around behind the drawn blinds. He imagined the carousing still underway, how nothing had changed in his absence.

Where the PKG house was tall, the Sigmas' was wide and long like a barracks. Tim had showed up once for a night of Jell-O wrestling that took place in what the Sigmas called The Garage, a large room off to the side of the house, all concrete and exposed caulk, no air conditioning or heat, just a large empty space where all the spilled beer and drunken antics could be contained.

He and Cal marched up the long drive, gravel crunching under their feet. Tim wasn't sure what they were doing, but Cal hadn't paused, hadn't hesitated when Tim continued to walk next to him. Unlike the PKG house, the Sigmas' was quiet, the front windows dark. When Cal opened the door, Tim couldn't hear a single bit of noise. They entered a tiny foyer where portraits of the Sigma founders were hung, along with the most recent fraternity composite; in the dark, Tim couldn't find Cal, and he didn't have time to dwell, as Cal was already turning down a long hall leading toward his room. The floor was scuffed and slick. Most doors were closed, and the few that were open were barely cracked, light spilling out through the frames. Twice, Cal called out in a stage whisper to someone and received the briefest of replies.

Finally, Cal stopped at a closed door and fished for his keys. He turned to Tim and said, "We've had a rash of pranks, so I keep my door locked now. Two days ago, someone stole all of my light bulbs."

"Your light bulbs?"

"They were hanging in my closet in a plastic bag."

"Funny."

The room smelled of leather and dirty laundry, earth and sweat. Almost like their locker room, but minus the overhanging stench of piss. The furniture was simple: a pair of twin-sized beds on opposite walls, a bureau, a tiny writing desk strewn with notebooks and pens and a snoozing laptop. Cal emptied his pockets onto the bureau and Tim stood with his back to the door, which Cal closed as soon as they were both inside. Cal sat on one of the beds and thumped the mattress next to him.

"What about Dave?" Tim said.

"What about him?"

"What if he comes back?"

"He won't." Before Tim could say anything, Cal added, "I told him not to."

"Oh."

"Asked him, I mean."

"Why'd you do that?"

"Just sit down, would you?"

Tim came and sat next to Cal, who reeked of beer and rum and the percolation of sweat, the latter of which was, instead of off-putting, cloying and sweet and intoxicating. It filled Tim's nostrils with want, the hints of exertion and effort, and he found himself leaning in Cal's direction. The back of his neck tingled, and his vision spangled just so.

Cal set his hand on Tim's thigh, and Tim felt himself getting hard, erection pressing against his jeans. His mouth was dry. The little blister of warmth he'd felt when Cal's fingers touched him in the locker room was now a full-on blaze, heat strumming in his cheeks and chest, his torso feeling scooped out, as if his viscera had been dumped on the floor.

"Hmm," Cal said, and then his mouth was on Tim's, saliva sticky from drink. Tim's lips were an iron line, his spine snapped straight, but when Cal's fingers dug into his quads, Tim relaxed, opened his mouth, and put one hand on Cal's shoulder, the muscle rippling beneath his shirt.

Cal moved his hands to Tim's belt buckle. Tim was going haywire, his heart thudding hard. Was he about to pass out? He wrapped one hand around Cal's wrist, but Cal didn't seem to notice. A waft of cool air passed over Tim's legs as his jeans came down. Cal let out an amused chortle at the tenting of Tim's boxer shorts, and suddenly he was gripping Tim through the fabric. Tim shuddered.

"Oh, yes," Cal said. He let go of Tim's erection and moved both hands up his shirt, dragging the fabric away. Cal removed his own, too, revealing the musculature Tim had so long avoided looking at despite the desperate itch inside him. Cal's nipples were dusted with blond hairs, as was his stomach, a trail that widened as it went lower, like the train on a wedding dress, spreading in a golden curtain toward his hips. His necklace winked in the moonlight. Cal placed both hands on Tim's chest.

"How did you know?" Tim said.

"Know what?"

"That I would—"

"If I was wrong, I was wrong." Cal trailed his tongue across Tim's throat. "Who cares?" His teeth gently gnawed at Tim's throat, hands on Tim's hips. Cal pushed Tim down onto the bed. Cal's knees surrounded Tim's. Tim reached out a hand and fiddled with Cal's belt and Cal watched his fumbling, trembling fingers.

"You haven't done this before, have you?" Cal said.

Tim's head moved in a half-circle.

"Is that a yes or a no?"

Yes and no; he'd had sex twice in high school, with a cheerleader who had followed him around doe-eyed for three years before she finally had the gumption to ask him to be her date to prom. He'd said yes, and they'd snuck out of the reception hall early, hopped in his car, and drove to her house; her parents were out of town. They did it twice, once that night and then in the morning, their bodies dewy and glowing and slick with perspiration.

"It's okay," Cal said, voice somewhere between soothing and sing-song. "Allow me, ERA."

"Please don't call me that."

"Why not? It's who you are."

"No it isn't."

"Then who are you?" Cal said. His breath was hot on Tim's throat. "Who do you want to be?"

"I don't know," Tim whispered. Cal kissed him again, flooding Tim with pleasure. His toes curled. He let out a shocked groan. His back arched. He thought he should tell Cal to stop, but why? He felt like a car engine popping with ticking heat after it's been turned off. He stared up at Cal's ceiling, noticing the Sigma flag tacked there for the first time, situated next to a ceiling fan whose blades glimmered dark brown in the moonlight. A large black sigma was embroidered in the center, a star on one side and a filled-in triangle on the other, both the same blood red color. He wondered what they meant. The fabric was pouched downward, held up at each corner by a trio of thumbtacks. Tim imagined them failing in their duty, flying down and piercing him in the eyeballs.

Maybe we're all freaks, he'd said to Cal. As if that was an explanation, some kind of invitation. He thought of the magic of his fraternity brothers, the things their bodies could do. Cal stopped kissing him on the mouth and moved his lips lower, along with his hands. Tim let out a long breath and let Cal do what he wanted. Maybe they could come up with a new name for Tim. Or maybe he could be ERA. Maybe he could be anything at all.

Frequent Flyer

At first we called him Teabag, not because he had any tendency to drape his balls on passed out partiers but because he only drank tea, even during keggers, carrying mugs of it around that he held with two hands, shaking off invitations to play Fuck the Dealer or Circle of Death. When the weather was a fug of heat, he held plastic tumblers full of Darjeeling over ice. Girls teased him, and no matter how much cajoling we did on bid night, he wouldn't guzzle the bottle of Cold Duck on the front porch, as was tradition for the new pledges, but we let it go because we prided ourselves on accepting people for who they were, even if refusing a complimentary Natural Light from a senior who hardly ever came around was the greatest sin one could commit, of which he was guilty on many occasions.

We then started calling him Frequent Flyer when we noticed he went out of town every weekend. It took some goading—especially because he was never drunk, tongue never loosened enough to release his deepest and silliest secrets like the rest of us—but he eventually admitted that his parents were rich. They'd wanted him to go to one of the Ivys or Stanford or Pomona, but he wheeled and dealed and convinced them to let him go to our sleepy liberal arts college just south of the Iowa border instead, and to use the savings to travel on the weekends, taking puddle jumpers down to St. Louis, where he'd board a flight to some off-the-beaten-path hiking trail or nature preserve or cultural vista that would provide deep personal growth. His part of the bargain? Maintaining a perfect GPA, never getting in legal trouble, and making enough connections with the mid-tier business department faculty to get a cushy internship that would hopefully lead to an at least marginally boast-worthy job in hedge fund management or investment brokerage.

His parents signed him up for a frequent flyer program and a credit card through one of the airlines, on which he purchased all of his tickets and hotel rooms. Sometimes, he said, he stayed in hostels, like when he went down to Guanajuato and the Nicoya Peninsula. He racked up enough miles to go to Rio de Janeiro, where he spent all of spring break while the rest of us drove back to our middle-Missouri suburbs to pick up shifts at jobs we left behind nine months out of the year or caravanned to the Gulf Shores and drank shitty, sugary concoctions on the beach. He came back every weekend with a story about some hole-in-the-wall restaurant or a majestic outcropping that overlooked a waterfall. He never took pictures, but he carried Moleskines with him when he traveled, jotting down notes and observations. We never knew what his major was—he seemed to take slapdash courses each term, a weird mix of art and history and English and chemistry—and he never went to the library. But he seemed to know something about everything, helping people out with calculus homework, business ethics papers, and microbiology labs. He was also a good pledge, memorizing the chapter's history, our founding date and names of the exec board. Even though he was gone so much, he learned the motto and could recite the entire Greek alphabet after one week; he said he'd taught himself the language when he was fifteen because he thought it was interesting and he wanted, one day, to go to Athens.

He kept a teakettle in his room. He filled it with tap water and carried it to the kitchen, which was situated in a corner of the house's basement, one wall a row of cabinets with combination locks on them so no one had their snacks and laundry detergent stolen. He would wander the house knocking on doors asking if anyone wanted a cuppa—that's how he said it, *a cuppa*—holding up the kettle and swinging it gently. He offered a variety of options from his store: Oolong, Pu'er, Jasmine, Yerba Mate, and when people said yes he nodded, trundled down the stairs, and returned fifteen minutes later with steaming cups on a tray that he polished every Sunday evening after chapter meetings, delivering exactly what had been asked of him to exactly who had asked for it. We added tea from the beehive in the backyard; Hot Lips rewarmed cups that went tepid, blowing little flames against the porcelain. Picasso always used the same saucer, his painted prints smeared along the edges.

"Don't you get tired of flying?" we asked, and he would shake his head. He loved arriving at an airport an hour before takeoff, slithering through the security line, playing the speed game of peeling off his shoes and belt and dumping his personal items into the plastic bins as fast as he could so as not to frustrate the business executives waiting in line behind him or the ragged parents trying to corral their sugar-loopy children. He loved nestling into a seat near his gate and pulling out a book, focusing on a few pages be-fore being distracted by the sights and sounds of fellow travelers, men and women with cell phones pasted to their ears power-walking past the Sbarro and CNN Newsstand. His greatest joy was finding his seat—always a window—and peering out at the employees carting up the luggage or refueling the jet or waving the small flags with gestures that were like a different language, then feeling the growl of the engine as the pilot revved up for takeoff, and then, of course, the feeling of lift in his stomach as the plane kissed away from the ground and his ears went stuffy from the sudden change in elevation and the earth zoomed out, buildings and farmland and highways turning to specks and colorful squares and gray ribbons far below.

He loved telling us about where he went. With a mug steaming in his hands, one foot curled under his body, the other tapping the floor, he would tell us about flying to Denver so he could cross the Continental Divide, the geography of America laid out like a banquet below. Or his trip to Petrified Forest National Park, sighting mule deer and black-tailed jack rabbits, to Pike Place Market in Seattle, where he took in the smells of fresh flowers and fish and bought a cup of mango cut right there. How he flew from St. Louis to LAX to Seoul and back, stopping in South Korea only long enough to take a bike tour and see the Gyeongbokgung Palace before turning around and flying out of Incheon International. Frequent Flyer's voice would rise in pitch as he told his stories, as he reveled in eating crawfish in Lake Charles and slurping hot bowls of caldos in El Paso. His cheeks would flush, joy warming his voice, and he would sip his tea, swallow, and tell us to add these places to our bucket lists.

But then it all stopped.

We knew something was up the night he came back to campus after winter break of his sophomore year and asked if someone would buy him beer. A dozen of us were sitting on the leather sofas surrounding a flat-screen television where we watched whatever shitty movies were on USA or TBS. We thought his request was some kind of test, and for a moment none of us said anything, a televised explosion the only noise. We looked at one another, our own cases of beer tucked between our legs on the floor, and finally a senior let out a yawn, slapped his thighs, and said, "Sure thing." They came back twenty minutes later, Frequent Flyer looking bizarre with a six-pack of Bud Light bottles cradled in his arms like one of those flour-bag babies that teenagers are compelled to care for, showing them the ravages of early parenthood and the risks of porking before you have a full-time job.

We watched him twist the cap off the first bottle and slip it carefully into his pocket like a delicate souvenir. He read the label, squinting at the surgeon general's warning and the ABV. Then he took a sip. His face betrayed nothing, as if he was simply drinking some English breakfast, long-steeped so its bitterness dragged across his tongue. We watched him swallow, his Adam's apple and the cartilage in his neck fluttering. Frequent Flyer said nothing, cupping the beer in his hand like his palm and fingers were a koozie. He sunk into the cushions, stared at the TV for a minute, and then drank another sip, letting the bottle linger on his lips.

He only drank two of the beers, taking the remainder up into his room, which he shared with a guy who always slept at his girlfriend's apartment several blocks from campus. We gathered near his room, listening, but he didn't emerge the rest of that evening. In the morning, he looked haggard, as if he hadn't slept. We gave him gentle ribbing about a hangover, but he hardly responded, swatting away our jokes as if they were mosquitoes buzzing at his ears.

We watched him fall apart. When he stayed that first weekend, the eve of the new semester, he drank his tea as usual, offering to bring us our own steaming cups, but he mixed up who asked for jasmine versus green or white, which of us wanted sugar and who didn't. He blinked at us when we joked that he was going soft, and we noticed darkness beneath his eyes, how puffy and red they'd gone, as if he'd spent the previous night crying through the wee hours. During that night's party, he brought down the rest of his six-pack and drank three of his beers, lifting the bottles to his lips with a hitchy slowness, like he was an infant finding his legs.

We eventually figured it out: his father was in legal trouble, something about taxes and off-shore bank accounts, the kind of thing we saw on police procedurals and in the B-movies we watched in the afternoon. His credit card, with all those miles, all those promises of future flight, no longer worked, and his parents were getting divorced, his mother leaving, not because of destitution but because of the dishonesty. Frequent Flyer had earned himself a merit scholarship, so he could still go to school, but he would have to find a job to pay his rent, which was only a few hundred bucks a month because living in our house was cheap; the rooms were small and the kitchen in need of a remodel. He said all this in bits and pieces, his voice slurry as he mumbled the truth to whoever was nearby. We didn't know what to say beyond "Jeez" and "That sucks, dude," but most of us didn't say anything at all, instead slapping him on the back and offering a cheers, which he accepted with the dulled automation of a robot in need of a good oiling.

We watched him with worry, our necks going tingly when we saw him stumble out of his room past noon; we knew he had morning classes. His hair was tangly and his body stank. He never asked for more than a six-pack of beer, of which he would maybe drink half in a night. Sometimes he still made tea, and we wondered if we should start calling him Teabag again, if Frequent Flyer was like a fresh stab wound, a ripped-open scar, every time we used it. But we also didn't want him to feel the renewed sting of loss, as if our nickname for him was the last thread of a life he no longer possessed. As if, somehow, if he was still Frequent Flyer, it might all come back to him. Instead, those of us with eight AM classes started knocking on his door before we trooped onto campus, demanding he get up, drink himself some black tea, and start his day. We pulled him along to the library on Friday afternoons, forgoing our end-of-week pre-partying in the front yard for the sake of salvaging his grades. He fidgeted, taking twice as long as he should have to complete his Latin translations or his History of Sub-Saharan Africa papers (we still had no idea what his major was), but he got the work done. We started asking him for tea, and some of us began carrying our own steeping mugs down to parties, blinking and shrugging when our friends said, "What the hell?"

"It's tea," we would say, sipping and staring over the lips of our cups as we drank, inhaling the sharp scents of hibiscus or chamomile or rooibos. They ragged us, wanted to know why we weren't taking shots or shotgunning beers, how we could play beer die with bone china or porcelain. We shrugged and said, "Maybe not tonight."

Soon enough, we were all drinking tea, even when we went to keggers, carrying our own plastic tumblers full of iced chai or lukewarm peppermint. On Sundays, we drank TAZO Dream and got strong, eight-hour sleeps, waking up fresh and ready for our econ tests and marketing presentations. Frequent Flyer watched us when we asked to borrow the teakettle and crowded around the stove in the kitchen, which we cleaned, holding our noses when we opened the communal fridge so we could dispose of the funk-laden Tupperware containers and curdled milk in its plastic gallon jugs. We bought fruits and veggies, started sautéing with the non-stick skillets we deep-cleaned in the industrial-size sink.

"This is nice," we said to each other.

"It's great."

When spring break rolled around, some of us organized a road trip to Clemson, South Carolina, home of our founding chapter. We asked Frequent Flyer if he wanted to come, and we saw the yearning in his eyes, but he shook his head no. "I have to go home to work," he said.

"Work?"

"My parents are both broke," he said. We waited for more, but nothing else came.

Finally, someone said, "Will one week do that much? You need a break."

Frequent Flyer closed his eyes. We were sitting on the couches on a Tuesday afternoon, drinking our tea and watching *Jeopardy!*, yelling out ridiculous answers when no one knew the right one. Someone had bought a tray of cucumber sandwiches from Hy-vee and a spread of petit fours. We'd stripped a bed of its top sheet and laid that over the coffee table so we could pretend we were refined, enjoying a true afternoon high tea. We had no kidney pies or pickled salmon, and no one had any idea how to make onion cakes, but when Frequent Flyer had seen the setup, he'd laughed, tossed himself down on the couch, and picked up the mug we'd prepared for him. But now his jaw was set, his gaze fixed on the screen, where the Final Jeopardy category—English History—had just been revealed, Alex Trebek sending the show into its final commercial break. He sat silent and stony except for the hinge of his arm as he lifted his teacup to his mouth and slurped.

"I've taken plenty of breaks," he said, finally. He set his cup down, empty. "I deserve some hard work."

We looked at one another. Frequent Flyer's hands were curled in his lap like a pair of nestled pups. He stared at the television, then barked out, "Anne of Cleves!" We looked at the screen, where the Final Jeopardy clue was scrolled over the screen: *This wife of Henry VIII outlived the rest of his wives when their marriage was annulled after six months, when it was declared unconsummated.* Frequent Flyer looked at us. "I went to Westminster Abbey freshman year. She's buried there." He picked up his teacup. "Lots of famous dead people are."

We went to Clemson without him, nine of us crammed into two cars, taking turns behind the wheel. We passed through Nashville and Atlanta, stopping to check out the Country Music Hall of Fame and Grand Ole Opry. We toured the Coca-Cola Headquarters, sampling soft drinks from around the world. When we ate dinner in Chattanooga, we all ordered sweet teas in Frequent Flyer's honor. We took photos out the car windows as we crossed the Savannah River and texted them to him, wishing he was with us. He didn't respond. In Clemson, we slept in a trio of hotel rooms that stunk of our beer breath and drunk sweats after two days. We wandered the South Carolina Botanical Gardens, drank cheap lagers in the bleachers at Doug Kingsmore Stadium. We found a tea shop and stomped through, buying up baggies of leaves we'd never heard of before: purple beauty, tomato mint, maple. We decided to make Frequent Flyer a basket full of the most exotic things we could find, adding comfrey and Labrador, along with a set of sparkling green cups.

At the end of break, we were tired and hungover from so many nights at Clemson's downtown bars. We skipped any sightseeing on the long drive home, stopping only to piss, grab burgers at drive-thrus, and screech onto the shoulder when someone needed to puke. But we were excited when we reached our familiar tiny town with its lawn supply outlet on the outskirts, its dusty gas station parking lots, fast food restaurant cups and wrappers trapped along storm drains. And the dogwoods along the edge of campus, the familiar gold of our fraternity letters lit up in the night atop our house. We piled out, careful to pull our basket of wares for Frequent Flyer as we brought our duffel bags and leftover beer in through the back door. We were all excited to give it to him, to watch him smell at the ground leaves, to hold the new cups and their saucers in his hands.

But he wasn't there.

Frequent Flyer's room was empty, not only him missing but also his bedsheets and textbooks and clothing; his closet was like a mouth with its teeth ripped out. We asked around the house if anyone had seen him go, but everyone shook their heads. Those who had stayed in town for break said that he was there one day, gone the next; he snuck out in the dead of night. We imagined him carrying his things downstairs, one pile at a time, and cramming them into his car. We dropped the basket in the middle of his room, letting it thud against the hardwood, the teacups rattling like they'd been clinked together in a toast.

The one thing he'd left behind was his teas. And beneath a canister full of Earl Grey we found a note, written in his simple, blocky handwriting. It was only three sentences: the first an apology, the second an explanation—he was leaving school to work full-time—and the third a goodbye. We stood around, looking down as if the piece of notebook paper was a dead body, and said nothing. Then someone said, "But what about his teakettle?"

We found it in the kitchen, sitting on the back burner. Frequent Flyer had polished it so that the steel shone; we could see our stretched shapes in the curved surface, reflections wonky like we were staring at a funhouse mirror.

We made tea. We set out sugar cubes, arranged the saucers on Frequent Flyer's tray, which he'd left on the kitchen counter, equally polished and fine. We imagined him working at a restaurant or a retail store, stuck behind a cash register or in a warehouse. We listened to the squeal of the whistle as steam erupted from its spout, imagined that it was the yearning cry he must let out from time to time as he worked, steeped in the loneliness of the walls and high ceilings and his sorry inability to break free, to see the world, to burst forth and take flight.

Mort

Lena McCuskey took Danny's virginity on a hot Friday afternoon an hour after last period. He'd pulled his car into a shady corner beneath the cherry blossoms at the edge of campus, his car half-hidden by the dumpster near the back door of the gym. It was all thanks to the car that he found himself splayed in the back, Lena pulling down his pants with one hand while managing to yank up her t-shirt with the other. He was sweating and trembling, his hands shaky as they reached up and cupped Lena's sides. Her mascara was running, not because she was sobbing with regret or fear but because of the melty heat; it grabbed her hair and slapped it against her face, like tendrils of dense, rotting seaweed. The car's interior was already humid like a greenhouse, the windows gathering condensation, which Danny could barely see thanks to their dark tint.

Danny drove a hearse.

When his parents bought the car, surprising him on his eighteenth birthday, a heavy snowstorm came through in the middle of the night. They brought him outside in the morning, blindfolded. He could tell his parents were proud of themselves, both grinning above their steaming coffee mugs, wearing their matching pajama suits and puffy slippers. They stood in the jaw of the garage while Danny tiptoed out into the driveway, his feet crunching through the chunky, ice-slicked snow. He uncovered the recognizable humped vinyl roof.

"Really?" he said.

His mother frowned. "It's what we could afford."

"The driver's seat is actually really luxurious," his father said. "It'll make you interesting and different."

Danny resisted the urge to say, *It'll make me a freak.* He knew his parents cared, that they worked hard. His father managed a Walgreens, and his mother worked at the local university's health center doing medical coding. They must have saved and discussed and searched and searched to buy him this car.

As if reading his mind, his father said, "We got a good deal."

"Thanks," Danny said. "Really. It'll be, uh, unique."

"That's the spirit," his parents said in tandem. They drank their coffee. His mother said, "Now let's get inside. It's cold. I'm pretty sure you have a snow day."

That cold was gone as Lena pulled off his underwear. Danny was semi-hard, and she took it in her hands without a word. When he'd first shown up in the hearse, his classmates had guffawed and elbowed him in the ribs, making jokes about how the goth kids would love it. Danny's parking spot—he'd paid for one at the start of senior year in the hope that he'd have a car before school was over—buttressed the walkway between the school's two buildings, and word of Danny's ride spread fast. The popular kids made jokes about Danny's parents changing careers (not that any of those kids had any idea what his parents actually did for a living) and one of the football players started calling him Mort.

"Get it?" he said one day, sidling up next to Danny at his locker. "For mortuary."

"Yes," Danny said, shoving his physics book into his locker. "I do."

"Oh, come on," the beefy red-headed linebacker with bloated arms and a beer belly said. "It's funny."

"Ha," Danny said.

The football player wandered into the scrum of students. Scuffed lockers opened and closed, students laughed and jawed one another, sneakers squealed against the tile floor. Danny threw himself into the din, marching toward his AP English class, where his teacher tried to get them to discuss Vonnegut's *Timequake*, asking what they would do if they had to relive the last ten years of their lives without being able to change anything, knowing exactly what was coming.

"Be pretty awful for everyone who died," Lena McCuskey said. "Imagine getting on an airplane you knew would crash."

Lena was the leader of the goth group. They all wore dark, monochromatic pants with t-shirts that looked like they'd been sucked through a wood chipper. Their lips were black, their eyes heavy with mascara. Lena's backpack was strangled with safety pins. She was smart, the English teacher's favorite despite the deadpan delivery of her conversation-halting comments. Danny had been paired with her as a junior in their college composition course. They'd written a partnered research paper on the Pennsylvania Turnpike murders, leaning over microfiche machines to read four-line blurbs from ancient copies of *The New York Times*. She'd been studious, not one for chit-chat, and had driven them to the St. Louis Public Library off Lindbergh because their dinky suburban branch, while full of paperback romance novels and a vibrant children's section, suffered a dearth of archival materials.

Lena's Buick LeSabre smelled of clove cigarettes and McDonald's fries. She didn't speak while they drove, nor did she play music. Instead she rolled the windows all the way down despite the cold that spun her hair into her face. She didn't push it away from her eyes as she navigated I-270, passing cars left and right, engine rattling as she broke eighty, then eighty-five miles an hour before, at the last second, at the Olive Boulevard exit, careening off. Danny had expected her to perhaps relish in the grisliness of the Turnpike murders, the mystique, but no: when she spoke, it was only to call out roll numbers and dictate how the order of events should unfold in their paper. They received an A.

She approached him months after he started driving the hearse, after his new nickname had spread like an infection. Everyone was calling him Mort, as if he were old and balding and clammy. Lena stood next to his locker just like the football player had, slouchy against the neighboring steel grille. Her hair was glossy in the hard light, so dark it looked like a wig, her pale skin like porcelain.

"I like your car," she said.

Danny blinked at her. It was the nicest thing she'd ever said to him.

"Could I check it out?"

"There aren't any dead bodies."

"Well that's disappointing."

Danny shut his locker. They started walking toward English.

"I think it suits you."

Danny wasn't a jock, though he did go jogging on weekends and grunted through pushups and crunches every morning, so he was in better shape than anyone would have guessed. He wasn't a band geek, or a drama nerd, or a gamer. He didn't count himself among the stoners, and definitely wasn't among Lena's goth crew. Danny liked to read, but he didn't carry thick tomes into the cafeteria. He had a smattering of friends from various cliques. His best friend went to the private high school a few blocks away, and on weekends they sat on one of their back porches, playing cribbage.

"After school, then?" Lena said when they arrived at the classroom door.

Danny nodded.

She said little that first time, looking over the interior, which was clean: beige leather seats, onyx accents on the dash and radio consoles. The casket rollers and bier pins were still installed, but Danny's mother had helped him cover them with some blankets and had even made jokes about him bringing girls back there; that's why she'd chosen a muted gray color: "We don't want the back to be too romantic."

Lena fiddled with the evergreen air freshener dangling from the rearview and then toyed with the radio, letting staticky whisper fill the interior.

"I expected it to smell like embalming fluid."

"I think they cleaned it pretty thoroughly before it went up for sale."

She stretched out her long legs. "Lots of space here, at least. What's it like to drive?"

"Like steering a boat."

"You've steered a boat before?"

"Metaphorically, I guess."

That made Lena McCuskey smile.

On their second afternoon together, Lena said, "Do you ever wonder about the bodies that have been in here?" She looked around as if doing an appraisal.

On the third occasion, she turned to look in the back and said, "Can we sit there?"

"Sure, I guess."

A stud winked in Lena's left nostril, and Danny asked about it.

"New," Lena said. "Did it last weekend."

"Did it? Yourself?"

Lena laughed. "I have a cousin who works in the mall. Does it all for free." She pointed up at her right ear, which was a panoply of stones and tiny gold hoops that munched all the way up to the cartilage at the top.

"Tough time getting through airport security."

"I've never flown anywhere."

"Really?"

She shook her head. The interior of the car was warm thanks to the sun. Lena's upper lip was dotted with the lightest bit of sweat. "My parents are homebodies. They went to fucking high school here. They live in the house my dad grew up in."

"Wow."

"What about you?"

Danny shook his head.

She kissed him then. Danny could taste the perspiration on her skin. Her breath was warm and smelled of strawberry. Her tongue plied at his lips and he opened them just so. He wasn't sure what to do, so he kept kissing her, his hands pressed against her sides, where he could feel trim, sinewy muscle.

When she gripped his erection, he shuddered and said, "Do we need—"

She shook her head. "I'm good."

"Good?"

She blinked at him. "I'm on the pill."

"Oh. Okay."

It was over quickly, which made Danny feel sheepish. Lena tilted her head and said, "That was your first time, wasn't it?"

He felt a flare in his cheeks, which were already flush from the heat inside the car, their bodies' mingled sweat, his panting breath. He could smell his natural aroma: salty and fuzzy and faintly tart.

"You were gentle," Lena said. "Boys stop being gentle fast." Her voice was different as she spoke, as if she was holding back something that she didn't want Danny to hear, a bit of broken glass in her throat. Maybe it was her real voice. Or maybe it was an invention. He didn't know for sure whether she was or wasn't who she made herself out to be. Lena pulled on her clothes and smiled at him, her teeth bright and clean. Danny was still naked. He tugged his pants to his crotch in a ball of denim, his underwear tangled in the legs.

"Don't worry," she said. "You were fine."

"Fine?"

"Trust me," she said. "That's a positive."

Then she crawled over the center console and sidled out the passenger-side door, letting a burst of afternoon air in after her, leaving Danny alone with the sticky air and a shuffling feeling inside him. He sat still for a long moment before pulling on his pants, his crotch swampy. When he dragged himself into the front seat, his foot caught on one of the rollers underneath the blanket and he flew forward, nearly smashing his face against the dashboard.

He gathered himself and turned on the ignition, leaning into the air conditioning that crusted the sweat on his forehead. Danny gripped the wheel, stared forward at the rotting wooden fence along the edge of campus that separated it from the neighboring private property. A strong afternoon breeze danced the branches of the trees looming above the fence. He felt spent, empty, tired. Instead of the starry endorphin-laced euphoria he'd always thought would come after sex, he felt a thick malaise, like he'd eaten too much.

He drove home in a daze. Every light was red. At each stop he felt the eyes of the drivers idling next to him sliding his way and—though he knew the hearse was the source of this staring—Danny was convinced he must look different, that the stink of sex must be vibrating out of him, illuminating his skin with a blinding alien glow. But when he glanced down at his hands, they were the same as always.

When Danny came through the front door, his father was slumped back in his BarcaLounger, grumbling at the television while he played video games. Danny didn't know any other parents who still dug Nintendo, and it was a seesawing point of both pride and embarrassment; sometimes Danny thought it was nice that his father felt youthful enough to navigate Mario and Link and Samus around on screen, but other times he thought he was the one who should be obsessed with those pixelated adventures.

"Happy Friday," his dad said. Danny's father was a big man; he'd played football in high school, though he hadn't been good enough for the college level. His face was always a shag of a full, thick beard, and he had hairy arms that seemed to go on for days. He wore endless polo shirts, even when relaxing in front of the television, but seemed to have trouble finding ones that fit his barrel chest; they were always too snug, practically bursting at his sides. Danny's mom, on the other hand, was a petite woman, tiny with sharp features and close-set eyes. Danny didn't really look like either of them but he knew this was how genetics worked: you were generally some weird amalgam of your parents. Even so, Danny looked at himself in the mirror and didn't see a single trace of either of them, nor any of his massive relatives on his father's side—he was lankier than any of his cousins or uncles—nor the more gnomish, stout members of his mother's family. His hair was somewhere between his dad's dark curls and his mother's straight strawberry blonde, and he had green eyes, unlike his parents' blue and brown.

"Some lucky recessive genes you got," his mom had said when he mentioned this. He'd smiled, but Danny had felt even more at sea.

His father paused his game and asked if Danny was hungry for a snack. His dad's schedule was a chaotic, unpredictable mess, constantly changing thanks to the unreliable twenty-somethings in his employ. He was perpetually on-call, forced to leap from the dinner table whenever some crisis came through on his phone. They'd once had to leave a Cardinals game in the middle of the fourth inning because his store had been robbed at gunpoint.

"No," Danny said. "Thanks though." He felt swampy in his crotch, the slime of sex still rotting on his inner thighs. He was sure his father would notice something was different; he was ob-servant, good at catching sight of would-be shoplifters. He'd ma-jored in English but had never managed to find a job where he could really make use of it. He had studied poetry and the Renais-sance, even had a small bust of Shakespeare that he kept on the fireplace mantel next to a trio of family photographs. His father didn't write much anymore, nor did he read, and Danny wondered if this was out of necessity or transformation, time and transition warping him into a different person than he'd been.

"Everything okay, bud?"

Danny nodded.

"You seem tense. It's the weekend." He finally seemed to realize that Danny had been late getting home. "Were you studying?"

"Some library research," Danny said.

"Studious. Good for you."

His father unpaused the game. His character, some kind of monk, stood in the middle of a dark forest, carrying a bō staff. Danny watched his father walk up to a lantern hanging from a tree branch and whack it with the staff, which started a small fire.

"Whoops," his dad said, sending his character running away from the growing flames. "Any exciting plans for the weekend?"

Danny shook his head. "I thought I'd catch up on homework. I have work tomorrow night."

"No parties or anything?"

"None that I'm invited to."

His father pursed his lips. "You could always throw one here."

"I don't know who I'd invite."

"Kids will come to a party even if they don't know who's hosting."

"Ouch."

"That did come out wrong."

Danny left his father on the couch and slipped upstairs to his bedroom, a small space with robin-egg blue walls and a bare dresser where he left spare change in messy heaps. He pulled off his clothes and stared at himself in the mirror hanging from his closet.

Danny's pubic hair was matted, his thighs were chafed bright red. He poked at his stomach and the curve of his nascent pecs. Aside from his gluey groin, he looked normal enough. This felt both like a relief and a disappointment.

On Monday, Lena asked if they could drive around after school.

"I have work at five," Danny said.

She raised an eyebrow.

"I wash dishes."

He'd taken the job after convincing his parents, who had wanted him to focus on school work, that his last semester of high school didn't really matter; his college applications were in, and he had nearly perfect grades (junior-year chemistry his lone B) and had done well on all of his standardized tests. He promised he wouldn't fail out in his last year, and he could use some spending money for when he went off to school. Danny hadn't told them his real goal was to work his ass off, take as many eight-dollar-an-hour shifts as he could so that, by the end of summer, he could dump the hearse and buy something else. Anything else.

He told this to Lena as he guided them through the grid of neighborhoods behind the high school, where brick-sided ranches and vinyl split-levels with basketball hoops above their garages were arranged in neat, wide streets with ample room for curbside parking. The car's acceleration felt heavy and elephantine through the gas pedal. Soccer moms unloading their kids and businessmen checking their mailboxes frowned at the hearse as Danny passed by.

"I can't see you washing dishes for a living."

"What can you see me doing?"

She shrugged.

They had sex again. Danny pulled up next to Lena's car, the hood smattered with samaras from the blooming maples. He could see a skull-shaped air freshener dangling from the rearview mirror. This time, she lay down in the back and pulled him on top of her. When she strummed her fingers down his torso along the small gulf at the center of his abs, she said, "These are a nice feature."

He wasn't in love with her; Danny knew that much. In fact, he wasn't even sure that sex with Lena meant that much to him. When Danny tried to remember the feel of Lena's skin beneath his fingertips, and what it felt like to be inside her, the way her body moved in response to his, it all felt like a distant memory. He could, if he concentrated long and hard, recall the fruity smell of her body and her sweat, the way the interior of the hearse almost went briny. But he didn't pine for her when they weren't together.

He kept waiting for something to happen: for Lena to disappear, for Lena to come sobbing to him that she was pregnant, for Lena to ask him to go on a real date. She continued sauntering the halls with her coterie of pale-cheeked, dark-lipped friends, their fingernails the color of tar, their eyelids bruised violets or violent, shrieking green, then meeting up with him after school. He would tootle her around like a chauffeur, zigging and zagging through town, making turns at random, always ending up back at the school, always moving into the rear of the car.

Graduation loomed. Senior superlatives were announced, and Danny braced himself for something ridiculous. None of the slots on the sheet that had been distributed in homeroom—Most Liked, Most Studious, Best Haircut—had seemed like a fit, but, he noticed, there was a space for miscellaneous write-in superlatives. When the class president's voice buzzed through the intercom system and read off the list—the football player was crowned class clown, of course—Danny never heard his name (somehow, no one on the student council had thought of Best Car).

He felt mostly relief, but bubbling underneath was a kind of sorrow. There weren't nearly enough superlatives for everyone; he wasn't alone in missing a wink of immortality. Watching his fellow unremarkable seniors, he saw not a trace of disappointment. They went about their business, slogging through the final days of the year with the same half-excitement, half-disdain as always. Danny wondered if he was the only one feeling the weight of anonymity, his unwanted nickname—even the horrible, half-senile AP history teacher had started calling him Mort—excepted.

On the last day of school, Lena said, "I don't even know where you're going to college."

Danny told her: one of the cheap state schools, where half of their class was probably going, too. Twenty-thousand students, a sprawling campus, gargantuan lecture halls and TAs that didn't care what your name was.

"What about you?" he said.

"I'm driving out to California for the summer."

"To do what?"

She looked out the passenger-side window, as if something interesting was happening in the nearby dumpster. "To be not here."

"It's that bad, is it?"

She smiled at him, which looked strange on her. "It's just not somewhere else."

"You don't want to go to college?"

"Someday. There's no expiration date. What are you going to major in?"

"I don't know."

"Well, what do you like?"

Danny looked down at his hands, surprised at their tight grip on the wheel as if he was in the midst of a high-speed chase. He relaxed his fingers. "I have no idea."

"You could be a poet," she said.

"My dad wanted to be a poet."

"What happened?"

Danny shrugged. "Life. Me, I guess."

"You could write poems about driving a hearse without dead bodies inside."

Danny chuckled.

"I'd read them," Lena said.

Graduation day came: sun bleary, humidity a thick gravy. Danny's armpits went soggy fast thanks to the unbreathable material of his cap and gown. Parents assembled in the air-conditioned gymnasium while the senior class gathered in the parking lot, students' faces flush, girls' makeup starting to smudge, the boys smelly despite their deodorant sprays. Danny stood in his spot between two people who were essentially strangers even though he'd been in at least one class with each of them every year; they spoke over him, as if he were a hedgerow or a park bench, about a party that night. He felt a tap on his shoulder, and when he turned, there was Lena, ignoring that everyone needed to be in their proper spot because the procession would begin any second now.

"Oh," Danny said. "Hi."

"Hi," Lena said. Her cap was fitted tight to her skull. Lena wasn't wearing heavy black lipstick for once, and her eyes were bare; she looked like a completely different person. How easily, he thought, she could transform herself.

"I have something for you," she said. "A graduation present."

"You do?"

"Find me after, okay?"

"Alright."

The ceremony plodded along, the principal and dean of students saying the things they were supposed to say. The valedictorian gave a brief speech that everyone applauded. Danny fanned his face with his copy of the program; his gown's polyester was like a shroud. When he crossed the stage for his diploma, his parents whistled even though they weren't the type. His classmates and the strangers in the audience clapped politely for him just the same as everyone else. When he shook the principal's hand, Danny could tell the man had no idea who he was. He turned his tassel at the same time as everyone else.

At the end, his parents gave him a hug. His mother wore a plum-and-white dress, colors in vaguely floral slashes across her body. His dad's tie was cinched too tight. They looked like all the other parents, proud of their kids, wearing their slacks and holding their purses, beaming. As they left the gym, Lena caught his eye and he told his parents he needed a second. They glanced at each other and smiled.

Lena stood by her car. If her parents had come, Danny didn't see them.

"Here," she said, holding out a black picture frame. "Sorry it isn't wrapped."

"That's okay. What is it?"

"Read it."

He took the frame. Inside, printed on cream-colored cardstock, was a poem: "The Hearse Song."

"It turns out there are a few hearse poems," Lena said. "But I thought this one was funny."

Danny read: *Don't you ever laugh as the hearse goes by / For you may be the next to die. / They wrap you up in a big white sheet / From your head down to your feet.*

"Thanks," he said. "When do you leave?"

"Tomorrow, probably."

"That soon?"

"No reason to wait."

Danny nodded and held the picture frame to his chest.

"Thanks for this," he said.

"No problem."

"I guess I should go find my mom and dad," he said.

Lena nodded. "Take care of yourself." Then she got in her car and shut the door. Danny backed away so she didn't run over his foot as she pulled out of her parking spot. She paused, rolled down the window, and said, "Bye, Mort."

Danny should have hated her for saying that, but out of Lena's lips, it wasn't so bad.

Danny didn't know it yet, but in just two weeks, the engine in the hearse will putz out. The cost to replace it will be prohibitively expensive. He will spend the rest of the summer working at the restaurant, sloshing dirty dishwater onto his torso, his hands drying and cracking from the blasting heat. He will bank enough money to help pay for a used Civic that will remind him of Lena's clunker.

When he arrives at college, he will join a fraternity. He'll tell his new friends that, for a short while, he drove a hearse, and that his classmates called him Mort. His Phi Kappa Gamma fraternity brothers will start calling him that too and, just like when Lena said it, he won't despise them for it. He'll tell ERA and Hot Lips and Picasso about Lena and the poem she gave him. He'll find more hearse poems—by Ella Wheeler Wilcox, Francis Beaumont,

James Whitcomb Riley—and he'll do what Lena said and start writing his own. His friends will find them odd, but magazines will publish them. He'll wonder about Lena, but he won't ever hear from her again. He'll meet his first boyfriend. He'll have sex with him, and when they share their virginity stories, Danny will tell him about Lena and the hearse and they'll laugh. Danny will laugh and be warm and happy and he'll know, finally, who he is, and when he graduates from college, headed off for graduate school—for an MFA, not to become a mortician—he'll pull the framed poem down from its place on the wall where it has stayed with him for four years. He'll bring it with him into the next place, and the next, and the one after that.

He watched Lena go, sunlight flashing off her car's hood and windshield. He'd have waved, but he was holding the picture frame with both hands.

Acknowledgements

My first and earliest thanks goes to the members of the real PKG fraternity: the Delta Delta chapter of Pi Kappa Phi at Truman State University, a place I called home for six years while I finished two degrees. I've borrowed bits and pieces from many of the friends I had while living in the strange town of Kirksville, Missouri, so many of whom I am still lucky to call my friends today. You may not breathe fire or sweat paint, but you've left your mark on this book in ways you probably can't imagine.

A deep well of thanks is due to my parents and my sisters for their endless support, even if my sister, Jamie, won't stop asking when these books will be in her hands. To all of my other friends, especially my colleagues who have done their best to create an atmosphere in our hallway that is conducive to creativity when so much of our environment is corrosive, I am deeply grateful for your warmth and friendship.

Of course, all of my writing teachers of yore, from high school through graduate school: you've each contributed a little piece of yourselves to making me, a gift I am eternally thankful for.

To the editors who first published a number of these stories, making me believe that a collection was possible. And of course to Christian, for your incredible and judicious edits and suggestions:

they took this book from collection to cohesion and I'm so grateful for the work you put into this manuscript. A shout out, too, to Dusty Marchand for the wicked, delicious cover art that captures this book's taste with such pin-point accuracy.

And last, to the cats: you're not as bad as that dedication makes you sound.

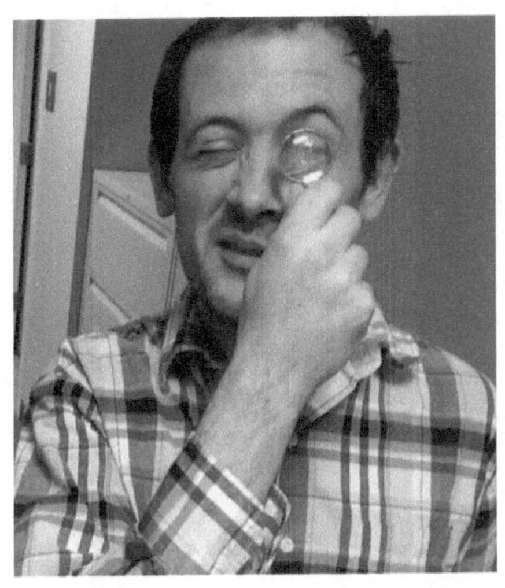

JOE BAUMANN is the author of *Sing With Me at the Edge of Paradise,* which was an Iron Horse Prize winner. He possesses a PhD in English, with an emphasis in Fiction Writing from the University of Louisiana at Lafayette. Baumann has served as the editor-in-chief of Rougarou as well as The Southwestern Review. He completed his B.A. and M.A. in English at Truman State University in Kirksville, Missouri.

Joe teaches writing at St. Charles Community College in Cottleville, Missouri, coordinating the program in creative writing, which offers an Associate of Fine Arts in Creative Writing degree as well as Certificates of Specialization in Creative Writing and in Literary Editing and Publishing. He has also serves the department's interim chair.